The Swiss Enigma
Secrets of the Alps

Secret Societies and the Sisterhood Sleuths

Cathy Warshaw

All illustrations (interior) by Oksana Ponomar

ISBN: 979-8218-99953-7 (paperback)
ISBN: 979-8-89766-834-2 (hardcover)
ISBN: 979-8-89901-759-9 (ebook)
ISBN: 979-8-89766-824-3 (audio book)

Disclaimer
This book is a work of fiction. While some locations, events, and individuals are inspired by actual events, places, and figures, all characters have been fictionalized. The events depicted in this story are entirely fictional. For all other characters, any resemblance to real persons, living or deceased, is purely coincidental and unintentional.

To my mother, you are my unwavering pillar of strength.
Your constant support has been the foundation of my journey.
Your belief in me has fueled my dreams and given me
the courage to pursue them with passion and determination.
Thank you for being my cheerleader, and my greatest inspiration.
I am eternally grateful for the beautiful love and support
you have given me.

To join the

Secret Societies and the Sisterhood Sleuths club

go to

https://www.sisterhoodsleuths.net, or

https://www.sisterhoodsleuths.blog

CONTENTS

Prologue

Arrival in Zurich

Snowflakes danced like tiny whispers through the air as the bus wound up the narrow, snow-lined road toward their lodge in Zurich. The mountains on the horizon were silent, cloaked in white, their jagged peaks hidden behind thick grey clouds. It was a place where secrets liked to sleep, buried deep beneath the ice and stone.

But something had awakened.

Inside the warm bus, Chloe sat by the window, her breath fogging the glass. She watched the snow swirl, her fingers absently tracing the outline of a coin tucked in her coat pocket. A coiled serpent—a symbol they'd seen before … one that haunted her now. Her intuition—a deep niggling feeling—was whispering in her heart that this meant something. Something big.

Next to her, Lily stared ahead, eyes sharp. Though younger, Lily had changed. Her eyes missed nothing now. She held the silence like a blade, ready to use it.

Their journey had begun in Upland, California, in hidden tunnels below where a strange object—the Obsidian Eye—had brought their ordinary lives to a crashing halt. That eye had led them across the world to Israel, where they uncovered the truth about The Society—a shadowy group that had controlled history from behind closed doors for centuries.

In Israel, they'd found the Seven Seals—ancient relics tied to an old prophecy that could change the course of the future. The Society had been after them, too. But Chloe, Lily, and the rest of the team had fought through danger, betrayal, and near-death escapes to stop The Society from using the seals to rewrite history and reality itself.

Now the seals were safe. Hidden deep within Switzerland's strongest vaults. Unreachable. Untouchable.

Earlier, they had traveled in silence to Zurich's financial district. Towering banks stood like fortresses made of glass and steel. Inside, everything gleamed. The air was colder. Franz Heissler had led them past security gates, deeper into the underground levels where the vaults rested behind thick doors that could withstand a war.

One by one, the seals were stored away. Locked. Forgotten.

But now, it wasn't just about the seals.

This time, it was about the Enigma. While the seals were now safe, The Society was not finished. And the Enigma … whatever it truly was … still waited, sleeping beneath the snow and stone.

Their next step wasn't to hide.

It was to search.

The bus came to a halt beside a quiet lodge nestled between thick pine trees. Smoke curled gently from the chimney. The place looked peaceful, like a painting from a winter postcard—but Chloe knew better than to trust appearances.

The door opened with a hiss, and Gil stepped out first.

The air changed.

He moved like someone who'd been trained to scan every shadow. Dark, wavy hair curled against his collar, and a leather jacket fit snugly across his broad shoulders. His eyes, full of secrets, swept across the snow-covered landscape. He didn't say much. He didn't have to. Gil had once led elite teams into enemy territory. Now he protected this one.

Chloe followed him out, then Lily, boots crunching in the snow. One by one, the others joined.

Luca arrived with his usual grin, curly hair bouncing as he swung his laptop bag over one shoulder. "Hope the mountains missed me," he joked.

"You're lucky we didn't," Chloe replied dryly.

Behind him came Yuki, her small frame bundled in a grey coat. She didn't speak, but her silver case was clutched tightly in her hand. Whatever was inside, it could probably crack a satellite system with a single button.

Then Mei stepped out, calm and composed, always watching. In Israel, Mei had discovered how far The Society was willing to go—using science and synthetic chemicals to change people from the inside out. She never said much about what she saw. But sometimes, Chloe caught her staring into the distance, as if remembering something she wished she could forget.

Next came Thalia, tall and graceful, her leather notebook tucked safely under her arm. She had deciphered ancient languages in Israel, uncovered tombs and forgotten ruins. There was wisdom in her quiet ways, and strength in her stillness.

Seraphine emerged from the bus, her hair falling gracefully across her back. She was like a ghost wrapped in silk. When danger neared, she was always the first to move—and the last to leave.

And finally, Aoife stepped down, towering above the rest, her Irish brogue echoing in the crisp air. "Well, this beats chasing seals in the desert," she said with a grin.

Lily smiled faintly. "Barely."

The team filed into the lodge, where warmth wrapped around them like a thick wool blanket. Inside, wooden beams lined the ceiling, and a fire crackled in the hearth. Klaus and Ingrid, the elderly Swiss couple who owned the place, greeted them with kind smiles. Klaus spoke little, but Ingrid handed Gil a white envelope as soon as they entered.

"They're already looking," she whispered.

The team gathered by the fire that night, tension tight on their shoulders. Maps were rolled out, old files spread across the long wooden table. Dr. Levine's letter was read aloud again.

The Society is not finished. They're also after the Enigma you've recently been told about—it is real. And they are closer than ever before.

What was the Enigma?

A puzzle. A truth. A secret buried so deep that no one had dared speak of it for centuries. Rumors claimed it had been hidden by Templars. Others believed it was connected to the beginning of Switzerland's secret banking system—an object or idea powerful enough to change not just wealth, but belief, memory, culture.

Two mysterious men had met them earlier, Hans and Fritz Müller. They had asked for the team's help to combat The Society's next move.

"The Society is still planning something," Gil said quietly.

"Worse than the seals?" Luca asked.

"Different," Chloe answered. "But just as dangerous."

In Israel, they'd barely stopped The Society from opening the prophecy hidden in the seals. But it had only been part of the plan. According to Dr. Levine,

The Society had been preparing for decades. They'd moved ancient gold beneath the Alps. They'd erased records. They'd recruited spies inside governments. And whatever the Enigma was … it was another part of their plans.

If they found it, they wouldn't need the seals anymore.

They'd still be able to control vast and dangerous power.

But the Sisterhood Sleuths weren't going to let that happen.

Chloe reached for the coin again, feeling the weight of its symbol.

The Serpent.

"This means something, I just know it," she murmured.

Gil's eyes narrowed and flicked to her hand fingering the coin. "Then we'll figure it out, that's what we do."

Not all treasure is gold. Not all power lies in weapons or money. Some power is hidden in what people believe, in the stories they forget, in the truths buried deep underground.

And now, in the land of the Alps, where their breath frosted in the air, the Sisterhood Sleuths turned toward the next mystery.

The Enigma was stirring.

And so were they.

Chapter 1

Unravelling the Enigma

The cold wind whipped through the twisting alleys of the Old Town, carrying with it the scent of roasted chestnuts and secrets. Cobbled streets echoed beneath their boots as Chloe, Lily, and the rest of the Sisterhood made their way to a tiny café tucked between two stone buildings. Its windows glowed golden, a warm beacon in the grey afternoon.

Inside, a man with silver hair and eyes like a glacier sat alone at a corner table, stirring a cup of espresso with an old silver spoon. He looked up just as the bell above the door jingled.

"That's him," Lily whispered. "Professor Felix Müller. He was the older gentleman we met earlier. His son was Hans."

He stood slowly, tall and proud despite his age, his face lined with stories. "Miss Lily," he said, with a bow. "The pleasure, I assure you, is entirely mine."

Lily smiled nervously. "We're glad to see you again. We gather you're the expert on … things that don't like to stay in the history books."

"And you've stirred up quite the ghost," he replied, his voice deep and smooth, like an old cello.

"We found something," Chloe said, sliding into the seat opposite him. She placed a photo on the table. It was of a feather, but not an ordinary one—it shimmered faintly in the light, and strange symbols ran along the shaft like ancient runes. Arthur had given it to them before they'd left for Switzerland.

Professor Müller's eyes locked on it. "That writing … that's pre-Roman. Very rare. This feather—it's not just a clue. It's a warning."

Everyone leaned in.

"We think it speaks of a chamber," Lily said, her voice low. "A hidden place. And a lost treasure called the Swiss Enigma."

Müller sat back, as if the words alone carried weight. "The Swiss Enigma," he echoed, almost reverently. "A phrase that hasn't been heard in years. Most believe it's just a myth—something whispered in secret among the oldest historians. But I know better. That's what I need to tell you about."

A shiver ran down Mei's spine.

"What is it?" Yuki asked.

"A legend," Müller said, lowering his voice. "One older than Switzerland itself. They say long ago, before banks and neutrality, this land held something ... dangerous. Powerful. And sacred. Something hidden."

Thalia's eyes narrowed. "Hidden by who?"

He glanced around, then leaned closer. "A group. Ancient. Older than any government. They called themselves *Custodes Umbrae*—the Keepers of the Shadow. They protected artifacts that could shift power, twist truth, even control fate and time itself."

Chloe frowned. "So the feather ... is one of those artifacts?"

"No," Müller said. "It's a message from them. A trail marker. Which means ... someone wants it found. Or ... someone's already hunting it."

The Shadow of the Past

The café dimmed as clouds covered the sun. Müller's voice dropped, and the Sisterhood huddled closer.

"Hundreds of years ago," he began, "this land was ruled not by kings, but by wisdom—druidic clans who read the stars and moved mountains with knowledge alone. When invaders came, they didn't fight. They vanished—into the land. Underground."

"They hid their power?" Luca asked, intrigued.

"They buried it," Müller said. "Literally. Under ice, beneath cities, inside vaults made of myth and stone. And over time, new groups formed—secret ones. Sworn to protect those ancient truths. But where there's power … there's always greed."

"And The Society?" Aoife asked, her voice tight.

Müller gave a slow nod. "They've been searching for the Enigma for generations. Using money. Politics. Fear. And now, they might be close."

"What about the symbols?" Seraphine asked. "We've seen them before—on walls, in caves, in places they shouldn't be."

Müller's face grew grim. "They're warnings. Traps. And sometimes … maps. If you found one, you're already in deeper than you know."

Lily's hand brushed the feather photo. "But what does it all mean?"

Müller looked each of them in the eye. "It means you've been chosen. Or … baited. Either way, the path is set. The question is, do you walk it?" He handed Chloe a slip of paper. "If you choose to meet this challenge, go here next, my son Hans will meet you. He's ex-Swiss Guard and very involved in this fight against The Society. He'll point you further."

The Journey Begins

The moment they stepped out of the café, the world felt different—sharper, colder, more alive with intrigue. Snow flurried down from the eves of buildings, dusting their coats like confetti from the past.

"No going back now," Thalia said with a wry smile.

Chloe stared at the photo in her hand. "We thought we were solving a puzzle. Turns out we've just opened a door."

"More like a trapdoor," Luca muttered, checking over his shoulder. "And who knows what—or who—is waiting behind it."

They didn't speak as they walked. The streets twisted like riddles, and in every shadow, a watcher seemed to wait.

On the distant horizon, snow-capped mountains loomed like frozen giants, guarding secrets that refused to die.

The Sisterhood had uncovered something big. Bigger than they ever imagined. A treasure hidden for centuries. A society older than time. A war waged in whispers.

And a clue that might be the first step to changing everything—or unleashing something that should have stayed buried.

Their journey had begun.

And this time, it wouldn't just be about finding the truth.

It would be about surviving it.

Chapter 2

The Watchers in Scarlet and Gold

Hans – A Cloaked Ally

The café wasn't on any map.

It didn't appear on tourist guides, TripAdvisor, or even Luca's shadowy collection of underground forums. In fact, it seemed determined not to be found, hidden beneath the rusted belly of an old clocktower that groaned every hour like it had indigestion.

The sign above the door simply read: *"Zytglogge."* No hours. No menu. Just an ancient-looking doorman who examined each of them like he was trying to remember their sins.

Lily leaned toward Chloe as they approached. "You sure this isn't some secret cult coffee shop? We're not about to be served human bone cappuccino or something?"

Chloe rolled her eyes, tucking a strand of blonde hair behind her ear. "It's a lead. We follow leads."

"Leads," Lily muttered. "Right. That's what we're calling potential death traps now."

Inside, the café looked like it had been decorated by a librarian with severe trust issues. Low lighting. Velvet chairs. Walls lined with leather-bound books and antique weapons—pikes, bayonets, and the occasional suit of armor peeking ominously from shadowed corners. The scent of old parchment and melted chocolate mingled in the air.

And there, in a back alcove near a fireplace that flickered suspiciously even though no logs had been added, sat Hans.

He wore a tailored grey coat that looked just shy of military, polished boots, and a burgundy scarf wound like a secret. His salt-and-pepper hair was neatly combed, and on his left hand, he wore a worn ring emblazoned with a tiny red cross.

He didn't rise to greet them. He merely lifted a steaming mug in salute and said, "You're late. Good. That means you're cautious. You'll live longer."

Luca was the first to speak. "Charming. Do all ex-Swiss Guards open with passive-aggressive tea-time threats?"

Hans' grin widened. "Only for hackers who smell like espresso and mischief."

Luca looked pleased.

Chloe slid into the chair opposite Hans, trying not to show how fast her heart was beating. "You've been watching us ever since we arrived in Switzerland. Haven't you?"

Hans nodded, unbothered. "Of course. It's my job to watch."

Gil took the seat beside Chloe, eyes sharp. "You're no longer with the Guards. Why are you still watching?"

Hans leaned forward, voice dropping. "Because not all oaths are made with words."

There was a brief silence, broken only by the hiss of steam from a hidden kettle.

Hans' eyes flicked to each of them in turn. "You've stirred something, you lot. The kind of thing that doesn't like being disturbed. The Society knows you're here. So do the ones who pretend they don't serve it."

Thalia, perched on the armrest of a chair, looked up from the silver spoon she'd been absentmindedly twisting between her fingers. "Then why help us?"

Hans took a long sip of his drink—definitely not bone cappuccino, Lily noted with mild disappointment. "Because I remember when we were the good guys."

That stopped them.

Chloe was about to ask more when Mei beat her to it.

"So you're ex-Swiss Guard. They protect the Pope … What do you know about the Vatican's biological storage?" she asked, her voice like silk laced with acid. "The lower levels. Where records are burned instead of filed."

Hans smiled at her like a grandfather tolerating a particularly precocious child. "Smart one, aren't you? Those records aren't just burned. Some are … consumed. You'll find the truth is rarely archived. It's usually buried. Or eaten."

Chloe's eyes narrowed. "By whom?"

Gil's hand brushed the back of her chair, protective.

Hans leaned back. "Let's just say the Vatican's appetite is older than the Church itself."

Yuki, silent until now, opened her compact black case and pulled out a tiny drone—no larger than a bumblebee. It blinked once. Twice.

"Does the Vatican still rely on analog surveillance?" she asked flatly.

Hans actually laughed. "Clever girl. Yes and no. You'll find technology behaves strangely in the oldest parts. Like something's … resisting. We used to call it The Pulse. Never lasted long, but long enough to kill a feed or make a man vanish."

Aoife crossed her arms. "Does the ground feel wrong to you here? I don't mean the city—I mean the earth here in Switzerland, beneath it."

Hans' gaze sharpened. "You're the one with the stones. You listen."

"I do," Aoife said simply.

"Then listen closely in Luzern. There are things moving beneath that city and the lake that haven't seen daylight in centuries."

Seraphine's tone was skeptical. "You're saying the Swiss Guards aren't just ceremonial? That you protected something … older?"

Hans didn't blink. "We were trained to do more than parade. The uniforms are a distraction. People look at the colors, not the shadows behind them."

Thalia tilted her head. "This feels bigger than just old secrets."

Hans looked genuinely amused. "That's because it is. You think The Society wants gold? Power? Control?"

He lowered his voice to a whisper. "They want certainty. To erase every unpredictable variable in the world—art, memory, love, history. They want the past so tightly wound they can choke the future."

"Creepy," Lily muttered. "Like, an evil version of Marie Kondo."

Everyone turned to look at her.

"What?" she shrugged. "You know. If it doesn't spark control, burn it."

Gil leaned forward, fingers laced. "So what is the Heart of the Alps? It's a phrase we've picked up on. It has something to do with this 'Enigma', doesn't it?"

Hans' expression sobered. He reached into his coat and pulled out a square of thick parchment, folded in quarters. He set it on the table with reverence.

"Once," he said softly, "there was a time when neutrality wasn't political. It was magical. The Heart is the source. A crystal—red as molten fire—that pulses with ancient energy. They say it controls the balance of Switzerland. Keep it hidden, and the country remains untouched. Reveal it—and chaos unfolds. And we suspect there are more than one."

"Typical," Luca muttered. "Why is it always magical glowing stuff?"

Chloe reached out and gently unfolded the parchment. A map, hand-drawn in staggering detail, revealed a series of interlocking tunnels beneath Luzern. Symbols, runes, strange markings in old Latin. In the center: a red dot. And one word.

"*Custodes.*"

The Keepers.

"What do we do with this?" Chloe whispered.

Hans' eyes gleamed. "Find the entrance. Solve the cipher. And don't go alone. The moment you open that door, the past will stop pretending to sleep."

There was a pause.

Then Hans stood, wrapped his scarf tighter, and placed a gold coin beside his untouched second drink.

"Next time we meet," he said with a wink, "bring biscuits."

And just like that, he was gone.

Zum
Goldenen
Widder

Chapter 3

The Plan Forward – What Lies Beneath?

A Meal in Zurich

Zurich at night was a snow globe of precision and secrecy, wrapped in golden streetlamps and blanketed in a calm that felt too orchestrated to be real. It was a city that smelled faintly of rain-polished stone, warm cinnamon from corner bakeries, and the unspoken rules of money. Not the loud kind—the kind that wore tailored suits and spoke in encrypted whispers.

They wandered the old streets like sleepwalkers, their bodies buzzing with the meeting they'd just left. Hans had vanished into the fog without a goodbye, and all of them were left feeling like puzzle pieces had just been handed to them without a box.

"We need food," Lily declared, tugging her coat tighter. "I'm serious. I'm about to eat my own scarf."

"You already chewed the end," Chloe pointed out, flicking her camera lens shut.

"Then I'm ahead of schedule."

They turned a corner and found it waiting for them—a small restaurant with golden lamplight pouring from the windows and a sign that swung gently in the cold air: *Zum Goldenen Widder*—The Golden Ram. A ram's head was carved into the wooden doorframe, polished by years of hands brushing against it.

"I don't care if they serve boiled shoelaces," Gil muttered. "If it's warm, I'm in."

Inside, it was like stepping into a storybook. Wooden beams crossed overhead like the ribs of a great ship. The walls were covered in copper pots, embroidered crests, and paintings of mountains so vivid they seemed to exhale mist. A fireplace crackled near the back, and the tables glowed with the flicker of beeswax candles.

The smell—oh, the smell. Butter, garlic, melting cheese, something sweet caramelizing in a pan. It hit them like a soft hug to the soul.

A woman with silver hair braided in a crown atop her head greeted them in German, then switched effortlessly to English. "You look like you need a place to think," she said, eyes twinkling. "Back room's quiet. This way."

"Do we have neon signs over our heads or something?" Lily whispered. "That's the second person today who read us like a children's book."

The back room was perfect. Cozy, quiet, just big enough for the nine of them to fit around a long oak table. The windows were frosted, casting a soft glow through the glass, and thick curtains made the space feel like it existed somewhere outside time.

Menus were handed out, massive and leather-bound, the kind that made you feel important just holding them. Everything was written in three languages—German, French, and Italian—though Luca's dramatic reading of a dish involving *"Geschnetzeltes"* earned him a quiet snort from Yuki.

"That's veal in cream sauce," she said. "Not a magical incantation."

"I was close."

"I'll have it," Gil said, shutting his menu with a snap.

Chloe scanned hers with curiosity. "Ooh, *raclette!* I've always wanted to try this."

"You're all getting the touristy stuff," Mei muttered, pointing to a page in the center. "This. *Capuns.* Swiss chard wrapped around spiced meat and herbs, poached in broth. Locals eat this. It's the real deal."

Luca perked up. "Sounds like food that's hiding something. I approve."

Aoife quietly ordered *Älplermagronen*—alpine macaroni with cheese, potatoes, onions, and apple compote on the side. Seraphine requested a dish with lake fish, her tone polite but distant. Thalia—after asking the waitress what she would get if she were sad and needed to feel alive again—ended up with wild mushroom stew and a slab of dark rye bread.

Drinks arrived first: spiced pear cider, fizzy elderflower water, red wine, hot chocolate so thick it could've been classified as a sauce. Then came the food—steaming, savory, and heaped in glorious piles.

For a while, there was blessed silence. Only the clink of cutlery, the occasional hum of satisfaction, and Luca's delighted moan over the *spätzli*.

"This is the best decision we've made since we didn't die in that museum basement," he said, mouth full.

"Please don't speak and chew," Seraphine said, pushing her fish around her plate.

As the food began to disappear, the table's mood shifted. The full stomachs softened their edges, but the weight of Hans' words hovered like steam above a hot pot.

It was Chloe who broke the silence.

"Hans said he's been watching us."

"Not in Israel," Gil added. "He didn't know us then, or did he? So … how?"

Yuki set her spoon down. "When we landed in Zurich, I noticed a flagged device near our gate. SwissGuard-OS. Military-grade operating system, but cloaked under a local telecom ID."

"You think that was him?" Lily asked.

"I think he's been tracking us since we pulled those bank files back in Upland," Mei said. "Maybe earlier. And he could've seen us on street cams, train stations. Zurich is a surveillance net."

Thalia was tracing the condensation on her glass again. "So he's not just some retired soldier. He's something else."

Aoife leaned forward. "He said he remembers when they were the good guys."

"He seems disillusioned," Seraphine said. "Which means he's either dangerous or exactly what we need."

Gil's eyes narrowed. "Or both."

The waitress returned, clearing plates and asking if they wanted dessert. They all declined, though Luca briefly mourned the passing of what he called "the rumored chocolate soufflé of destiny."

"We need a place to talk," Chloe said, her voice quieter now. "Somewhere not in public."

"I know the place," Gil replied. "Arthur set it up. East side of the city. Let's go."

Antiquariat &
Buchhandlung Gessner

Chapter 4

The Safehouse

If the restaurant had been a cocoon of candlelight and cheese, the tram that carried them away from it was a silver whisper of steel and silence. Zurich's trams didn't so much move as glide, their arrival so quiet it always gave the impression they were part of the city's nervous system—pulsing data, people, and secrets across cobbled veins.

They traveled east through the city, where the shadows grew longer and the houses older. Streets curled into narrower alleys, lined with snow-covered rooftops, small shops, and carved shutters that blinked like sleepy eyes in the cold night.

"Are we sure this is the right way?" Lily asked, squinting through the tram window. "Because it's giving … 'where fairy tales go to die' vibes."

Gil didn't look up from his phone. "It's the right way."

"How can you be so sure?"

"Because I checked it twenty-eight times."

"And once more for drama," Luca added, lounging dramatically on the back bench.

The safehouse, when they reached it, was the kind of place that didn't ask for attention—it repelled it. The storefront had once been a bookshop: *Antiquariat & Buchhandlung Gessner*, the letters faintly peeling on a sign above the beam. The display window held nothing but dust-coated volumes and a limp paper daffodil someone had folded and forgotten.

But the moment they stepped inside, the air changed.

It was warmer, heavier, filled with the scent of old pages, candle wax, and something faintly herbal—like thyme or memory. Bookshelves towered around them, stuffed with leather-bound atlases and forgotten maps, some curled and cracking with age. A cat (or what might've been a cat—it was unusually broad-shouldered and distinctly unimpressed) blinked once from its perch atop a stack of dictionaries and flicked its tail in approval. Or disapproval. It was impossible to tell.

"This is incredible," Chloe breathed. "It's like a library swallowed a fairy tale."

Gil strode toward the back of the shop and paused in front of a tall shelf filled with Goethe's works in every language imaginable. He pressed his palm against the spines of three particular volumes—Faust, Wilhelm Meister, and *The Sorrows of Young Werther*—and there was a low click.

The shelf creaked open with a slow, dramatic groan, revealing a spiral staircase that corkscrewed down into darkness.

"Of course it's a secret staircase," Thalia whispered. "Why walk through doors like normal people when you can descend into literary oblivion?"

The staircase ended in a long, stone hallway—chilly, but well-lit. The walls were lined with sealed crates, backup power cells, and faded posters from forgotten revolutions. At the end was a door with a biometric lock. Gil pressed his thumb to the panel, and the door slid open with a soft hiss.

Inside was the safehouse.

It looked like someone had taken a bunker and taught it to care.

The room was reinforced steel and polished concrete, but softened by thick Persian rugs, deep armchairs, bookshelves, and a massive wooden table scarred by history. Blankets were folded neatly on the back of each chair. A fireplace flickered in one corner, its flames almost licking at the edges of a map pinned to the wall above it. A kitchenette glowed in the far corner, complete with an espresso machine, a kettle, and several unopened bars of Swiss chocolate.

Luca walked in, turned a slow circle, and exhaled. "I take back everything bad I ever said about bunkers."

"No you don't," Seraphine said, brushing past him.

They spread out across the space instinctively—Yuki unpacking her gear on the table, Mei unrolling Hans' parchment map across the floor, Aoife taking a seat near the fire, her eyes closed as she listened to the ground like it might tell her its secrets.

Chloe stood in the middle, her hands on her hips. "Alright. Let's make sense of what we know."

"The Heart of the Alps," Gil began, pulling a marker from a drawer and circling the red dot on the map. "Hans said it's real. Not just a legend. If it exists, it's probably not just a power source. It's symbolic."

"Neutrality," Seraphine said. "Switzerland's shield."

Mei nodded, brushing her dark hair behind one ear. "And it's alive. The ink on this map responds to touch—but not everyone's. It pulsed when Chloe touched it."

Yuki leaned over the parchment, eyes narrowed. "That's nanobiological ink. Laced with microbial response layers. It's not ancient—it's cutting-edge. Someone has modern tech … guarding ancient secrets."

Aoife finally opened her eyes. "There's something beneath Luzern, like he said. Layers upon layers of structure. Roman foundations, medieval tunnels, modern vaults. All stacked like a *mille-feuille* of secrets."

"Oooh," said Lily. "Tasty and ominous."

Thalia drummed her fingers on the table. "We're not just talking about a rock with feelings, right? This is something The Society would kill for."

"They already have," Seraphine said. "We've seen what they're willing to do."

A silence fell. Heavy. Remembering those who hadn't made it.

Then Chloe spoke again, voice clearer this time. "So what's their endgame here? They've infiltrated banks. Vaults. The Swiss Guards. Why do they want the Heart?"

"Control," Gil answered. "If the stories are true, the Heart isn't just symbolic. It anchors Switzerland's stability. The Society doesn't just want to destroy history—they want to reshape the present. And the future."

"Unmake the world as we know it," Thalia added, a little too cheerfully.

"But how?" Lily asked. "What can one artifact actually do?"

Yuki answered without looking up. "If the Heart has electromagnetic properties—think geomagnetic influence, frequency modulation—it could affect everything from seismic stability to cognitive function."

Luca blinked. "Wait. Like … earthquakes? And mind control?"

"In theory."

"That's less neutral and more supervillain, no?"

"They're practically synonyms at this point," Mei muttered.

Gil paced. "We need intel. More than what Hans gave us. If we can get into the Luzern archives, maybe cross-reference energy signatures and historical seismic activity—"

"Or follow the tunnels," Aoife said suddenly. "The ones under the city and the lake. There's a convergence point. I'm sure of it."

Chloe looked at her. "A convergence of what?"

"Ley lines. Pressure ridges. Energy. Whatever's down there … it's waiting."

Yuki pulled up her tablet feed and flicked through thermal scans. "I've been running recon via satellite. There's a system of tunnels beneath Luzern, even running beneath the lake. Mostly sealed off, but one shows recent activity. Fresh heat signature. Last thirty-six hours."

"Whose satellites?" asked Luca, one eyebrow raised, "and how?"

Yuki just grinned enigmatically. "All of them. *I haf vays und meanz …*" she said in a creepy villain voice.

"Could be Society movement," Seraphine said, ignoring the banter.

"Or Hans," Gil countered.

"Or bait," Thalia offered, always helpful.

Lily had drifted to the far wall, where a board was covered in old photos, red string, and coded notes. She traced a thread that ran from Luzern, to a remote mountain area near a village called Guttannen, and then to Naples.

"This," she said, "started with the vault. The coded phrase. *'The Serpent sleeps beneath the city of Parthenope.'* What if this—Switzerland—is just a gate? A prelude?"

"What's Parthenope?" Lily asked.

"It's Naples," Aoife answered. "The city's ancient name. From when it was part of the Greek world."

Mei's eyes widened. "Then whatever's under Naples … is worse."

There was a pause.

Thalia suddenly gave a hoot. "Hey I know that village—Guttannen—it's really remote. Deep in the Alps. I've been there when on an information gathering expedition studying Nordic runes."

Then Chloe stepped forward, her voice steady. "Alright. Here's the plan. Tomorrow, we'll start by going to Luzern, there we'll split up. Luca, Yuki, and Seraphine will go to the Luzern infrastructure office and try to access old maintenance records. Look for hidden entrances. Anything that predates the official maps."

"I love breaking into bureaucracies," Luca said dreamily.

"Gil, Mei, Aoife—you'll trace the tunnel convergence points. Use sensors. Get ground readings."

"On it," Aoife said with grim delight.

"Thalia, Lily, and I will go to the Luzern Historical State Archives. Look for references to the Heart. Anything encrypted in folklore, old illustrations—"

"Or weird monks," Lily added.

"We meet back at a safehouse in Luzern at sundown—Gil will you arrange for somewhere for us to hole up? Try Arthur, or Hans."

Gil nodded. "And if something goes wrong?"

"We keep moving," Chloe said. "No lone wolves. No hero moves. We stay connected. We finish this. For everyone who can't."

"I'll get hold of Arthur and let Dr Levine know," Gil added, taking out his phone.

The flames in the fireplace cracked louder, as if the fire itself approved.

Outside, Zurich exhaled steam into the night.

And beneath it all, deep in the roots of the mountains and under the still water of Lake Luzern, something ancient stirred.

Waiting.

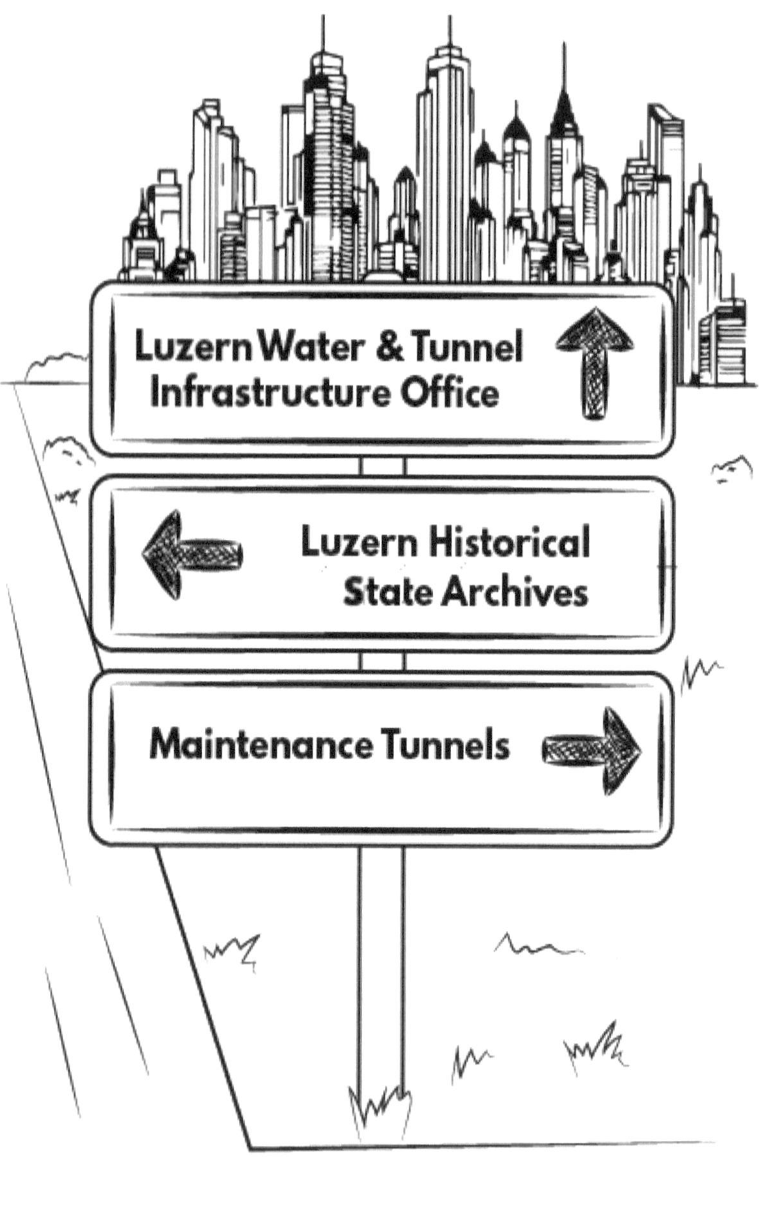

Luzern Water & Tunnel Infrastructure Office
Luzern Historical State Archives
Maintenance Tunnels

Chapter 5

Luzern – the First Mission

The morning broke cold and brittle. Mist hung low over Luzern like a silk scarf pulled across the eyes of the city, muting sound and smudging outlines. Even the trams moved more quietly, gliding like whispers along their tracks, as if the entire city had caught wind of something ancient beginning to stir.

After a short train ride to Luzern, the team had found their new safehouse the evening before, thoughtfully already prepped as was the one in Zurich, arranged by the ever-efficient Arthur and their new allies in Switzerland. A discreet former lodge, now permanently rented for their use, it stood surrounded by tall trees and a rustic wooden fence.

The Sisterhood Sleuths and their companions split at sunrise.

Each team had a mission. Each mission had a thread.

And together, those threads were drawing them straight into the spider's web.

Team 1: Yuki, Luca, and Seraphine – The Office of Shadows

Luzern's Water and Tunnel Infrastructure Office looked exactly like it sounded: bland, beige, and deeply suspicious.

It squatted behind the city's energy grid like a forgotten annex, with peeling paint, flickering fluorescent lights, and a receptionist who seemed to loathe joy. Or possibly people. Or both.

"I think she wants us to explode," Luca whispered, squinting over his shoulder as the woman gave them a look that could've soured milk.

"She wants you to stop flirting," Seraphine muttered, adjusting her scarf.

"I wasn't flirting. I was using tactical charm."

"Same thing," Yuki said, deadpan.

The plan had been simple: Yuki would patch into the building's systems from inside, using her palm-sized drone and a device that looked suspiciously like a compact mirror. Luca would stall any staff who got too curious. Seraphine would keep watch.

It was going fine, and they'd captured photos of a number of useful maps—until the lights flickered.

Yuki froze. "That's not me."

"What do you mean it's not you?" Luca asked from the hallway, his voice sharp.

"Exactly what I said. It's not me. Someone else is in the system."

Seraphine was already moving, slipping into the shadow of a filing cabinet near the door. "Luca. Eyes up."

Footsteps echoed in the hallway. Heavy. Purposeful.

A man in a dark uniform turned the corner, flanked by two others in matching jackets—no insignia, no name tags. Not police. Not city workers. Something in between. The kind of in-between that had authority but not oversight.

"Time to go," Yuki said briskly.

Luca sprinted for her as the uniforms barked something in Swiss German. She scooped up the drone and shoved it into her case just as he reached her.

"I don't speak angry," Luca panted, "but I'm pretty sure that wasn't 'have a nice day.'"

Seraphine, Yuki and Luca bolted for the side door, Luca hacking the lock with a code he'd memorized in three seconds flat. They burst into the alley as the door slammed behind them—and an alarm wailed.

From somewhere behind them came the sound of boots.

"Run now," Yuki said.

They did.

Team 2: Chloe, Lily, and Thalia – The Puzzle in the Archives

The Luzern Historical State Archives smelled like knowledge. And mildew. And something vaguely like pickles.

It was housed in a former monastery, complete with vaulted ceilings, stained glass windows, and a serpent carved into one of the door handles. Chloe liked it immediately.

"This place has secrets," she whispered.

"It also has mold," Lily whispered back, peering at a faded tapestry of what looked suspiciously like a goat jousting with a bishop.

They made their way down to the Restricted Collection, where Dr Levine's contact—an elderly historian named Dr. Eberhardt—had reluctantly granted them two hours of unsupervised access.

Chloe had her camera. Lily had a sketchpad. Thalia had exactly three sugar cubes she'd stolen from the café and was now pretending were magical wards.

It was there, in the back corner of the lowest level, that Chloe found them.

An old metal box, and next to it, a scroll. Ancient. Curled tight like a snail shell and tied with a crimson ribbon that had darkened with age. There were burn marks along the edges, and a symbol pressed into the wax seal—a coiled serpent eating its own tail.

"Ouroboros," Thalia murmured. "It's the snake. Always eating itself, birthing itself. End and beginning."

Chloe nodded and broke the seal.

Inside, the scroll was covered in precise handwriting. Dense. Meticulous.

And entirely in German.

Lily squinted. "Anyone here read angry calligraphy?"

"No," Chloe said, frustration prickling. "I took Latin in school. Not helpful."

Thalia tilted her head. "It's not just German. It's High Alemannic. An older dialect. And look—those aren't just letters. They're musical notes."

"What kind of lunatic writes a cipher in song?" Lily groaned.

"The best kind," Thalia said, delighted.

There was a chart—divided into squares like a crossword, with symbols along the top and left edges: a church bell, a ram, a mountain peak, a drop of water, a key.

Beneath it, a single sentence underlined in red ink: *"Der Gesang wird das Tor öffnen."*

Chloe didn't need a translator to understand it.

"The song will open the gate."

Team 3: Gil, Mei, and Aoife – Beneath the Earth

They descended through the maintenance tunnels like ghosts. No footsteps. No chatter. Just the echo of dripping water and the occasional creak of old pipes overhead.

Gil led the way, his flashlight cutting through the gloom.

"North by northwest," he muttered. "Two hundred meters. Then left."

"How can you tell?" Mei asked.

"Israeli special forces. We got lost in worse places."

Aoife trailed behind, one hand pressed to the wall. Her fingers moved in slow circles, listening.

"There's a shift," she said suddenly. "The stone changes here. It's not modern."

Gil stopped. "Show me."

Aoife pressed her palm to the floor. "Right here. Everything above us is concrete. But below? It's older. Carved. I suspect … stairs."

Mei knelt beside her, pulling out a sensor pad. It hummed softly as it scanned the ground. The screen lit up with a grid.

"There's a void below," she confirmed. "Three meters down. Roughly circular. No data on official records."

Gil ran his hand along the wall—and stopped. There, faint but unmistakable, was a mark. A carved outline.

A door.

Hidden beneath layers of cement and dust.

Aoife exhaled. "This is it."

Mei pulled a small vial from her pouch. Inside, a single drop of green liquid shimmered.

"Acid. Quiet but effective."

She poured it along the edges of the outline, and the cement sizzled. Slowly, a seam appeared. A line. Then a handle.

Gil braced himself and pulled.

With a groan like a waking dragon, the door creaked open—and behind it yawned a dark spiral staircase, descending into the mountain.

None of them spoke.

They simply looked at one another … and began to descend.

Team 1: Yuki, Luca, and Seraphine – The Chase

The alley behind the Tunnel Infrastructure Office smelled of damp stone and danger. Yuki's boots barely made a sound on the slick cobbles, but Luca's feet slapped louder, echoing between the buildings.

Behind them came the sound of pursuit—boots crunching, voices shouting clipped commands in German.

"They're gaining," Luca panted.

"No," Yuki replied calmly, pulling something from her coat. "We're just slowing down."

She flicked a switch on a small sphere the size of a walnut, then dropped it behind them. A second later, the device burst into a cloud of blinding white smoke.

They turned sharply into a narrow passage between buildings, almost invisible unless you were looking for it. Seraphine was already there, one hand pressed to an old, wooden door, her breath steady despite the sprint.

"In here," she whispered. "Move."

The door creaked open to reveal an old cellar, lined with dusty shelves and abandoned wine crates. They slipped inside just as the smoke outside began to clear.

Yuki shut the door behind them and placed a metal wedge beneath it.

"Will it hold?" Luca asked.

"No," she said. "But it will give us time."

Seraphine peered through a crack in the old wooden slats of the door.

Chapter 6

The Tunnels, the Cipher, and the Shadow

Team 1: Yuki, Luca, and Seraphine – Hunted

The cellar was musty, dark, and filled with the scent of vinegar and dust. It was somewhere secrets liked to sleep, curled between cobwebbed crates and forgotten barrels.

Outside, the voices were growing louder. The air felt like it was tightening around them.

Seraphine crouched by the crack in the door, her dark eyes scanning the alley through the wooden slats.

"They've split up," she whispered. "Two went east. One stayed behind."

"Cameras," Yuki said, already pulling out her case again. "We need to scramble the surveillance net."

Luca opened a nearby crate, revealing rows of wine bottles covered in layers of dust thick enough to write in. "If we live through this, I'm taking a bottle."

"You won't be alive to drink it if you don't shut up," Seraphine replied without looking at him.

Luca stuck his tongue out at her, moved the crate aside, and there was an old, metal box. Engraved on the lock was the familiar serpent eating its tail. He grabbed it and thankfully it fitted, just, in his pack,

Yuki connected her tablet to a cylindrical relay device, fingers moving like lightning. "Thirty seconds. I'm launching a phantom ping through the city's motion trackers. It'll look like we've gone toward the train station."

"Won't they notice it's fake?"

"Eventually. That's why we leave now."

Luca moved first, slipping through the back door of the cellar, gratefully leading outside into an even narrower lane. The fog that had blanketed the city that morning had returned, thicker now, curling through the alleys like smoke from an invisible fire.

They ducked into shadows, moved through backstreets, over iron fences and down a service stairwell that led to an underground passage.

"This way," Yuki said. "There's a tram tunnel under construction. It'll dump us near the bridge—less surveillance."

They moved fast, like ghosts skimming the edge of danger.

Above them, the city went on. But in the tunnels, something else had awoken.

Team 2: Chloe, Lily, and Thalia – The Cipher

The scroll lay unrolled across a table, held open with small brass weights shaped like lions. The red musical notations stared back at them like secrets waiting to be sung. They had tried looking in the small box but it was locked shut and no key was evident.

"Alright," Chloe said, biting her lip. "We know it's a cipher. A musical one."

"Can't we just hum it?" Lily asked. "I mean, how hard can it be?"

"Very," Thalia answered, tapping one of the notes with a fingernail. "These aren't just notes. They're tones mapped to locations. It's a geocoded melody."

Lily blinked. "A … what now?"

Thalia sighed and leaned closer, her voice taking on that peculiar mix of glee and frustration she reserved for arcane puzzles.

"It's a song that acts like a map. Each note corresponds to a physical location, or possibly an action. Like … play 'C' and a door opens in one place. Play 'F-sharp' and you release a deadly trap in another."

"Lovely," Chloe muttered.

Thalia pointed at the bottom corner of the scroll. There, hidden beneath what looked like a decorative flourish, was a tiny symbol.

"See that? It's an old musical key. Baroque era. But the rhythm—it's wrong. It's almost Morse code."

"Wait," Lily said, leaning in. "If it's code, I can help. I've been studying basic cryptography for fun."

"Of course you have," Chloe said, smiling. "Let's try it."

They worked for nearly an hour—Chloe taking notes, Lily translating, and Thalia humming the melody under her breath.

Finally, the translation came through:

"Where the water sings and the mountain listens, press the stone beneath the goat's shadow."

"That's not ominous at all," Lily muttered.

Chloe stood, the puzzle unraveling in her mind like thread.

"Luzern," she said. "The old chapel bridge—the *Kapellbrücke*. There's a carved goat statue on one of the stone supports. The Reuss River flows beneath it. I think that's where Gil, Mei and Aiofe's search will lead.."

Team 3: Gil, Mei, and Aoife – Beneath Luzern

The stairs spiraled downward, carved from stone that was older than language. It felt like walking into the bones of the earth.

Each step echoed differently—some with a hollow thunk, others with a deep, velvet thud. The air was cold, not just in temperature, but in feeling—ancient, untouched. Sacred.

Gil led the way, flashlight sweeping across the walls. Carvings lined the stone—runes, glyphs, and a peculiar serpent motif that repeated every few meters. It curled in different directions—sometimes devouring itself, sometimes splitting in two.

Mei ran her fingers over one. "These predate the Romans."

"You sure?"

"Positive. There's no symmetry. They're a language, but not one anyone's recorded."

Aoife dropped to one knee, pressing her palm to the floor.

"There's water below us," she whispered. "Moving slowly. Not a river. A pool. And there's … heat."

Gil paused. "Heat?"

"Not from the earth," she said. "From something else. Something … contained."

They reached the base of the staircase, and the tunnel opened into a chamber the size of a cathedral.

It took their breath away.

The walls were carved entirely from black stone veined with shimmering silver. At the center, a dais rose from the floor like an altar—and above it hovered a red crystal the size of a child's fist, suspended in midair by nothing at all.

It pulsed.

Mei stepped forward slowly. "Is that—?"

"The Heart," Aoife whispered.

Gil's eyes never left it. "It's alive."

Below the floating crystal, the floor was inlaid with thousands of metal panels—copper, bronze, maybe even gold—each etched with a different symbol. They formed a spiral that expanded from the dais, like the eye of a storm.

Mei pulled out her scanner. The device beeped. Then screamed.

"What does that mean?" Aoife asked.

"That it's broadcasting," Mei said. "Frequency unknown. Biometric pattern … human."

Gil looked up sharply. "You mean it's … calling to someone?"

"No," Mei said. "It's analyzing us."

Gil had known the moment they entered the chamber that it wasn't meant for people.

The air was too still. Too aware.

The Heart hovered in the center like a thought suspended in time—glowing red, faintly pulsing with something that wasn't electricity, wasn't magic, but sat somewhere between breath and memory.

"I don't like this," Aoife murmured. "It feels like we're being … observed."

Mei circled the Heart slowly, her scanner beeping erratically. "It's not just reacting. It's listening."

"To what?" Gil asked.

"Everything."

The moment her fingers brushed the edge of the dais, the air pulsed—and the metal plates beneath them lit up like a star map.

A spiral of light. Symbols. Coordinates. But not for this place.

Gil leaned over one.

"Naples," he whispered.

He looked at another. "This one is somewhere here in Switzerland. Somewhere in the Alps."

Mei's eyes met his. "More gates?"

The air shifted. The temperature dropped. And from the tunnel behind them came the unmistakable sound of footsteps.

Not boots. Bare feet. Soft, wet ones.

The three of them turned as one.

And in the mouth of the tunnel stood a figure—tall, emaciated, eyes too large and undefined like mist, skin waxen and stretched thin.

It wasn't breathing.

But it was watching.

All Paths Converge

At the safehouse that night, only Chloe, Lily, and Thalia had returned.

They were huddled by the fire when the encrypted comms buzzed. Chloe grabbed it.

"Gil?" she asked, relief flooding her voice.

"We found it," he said. "I think we're probably somewhere below the Reuss River. But we weren't alone."

"What do you mean? Found what? Who else is there, The Society?"

"I mean twe've woken something up. And it remembers being buried."

Then the comms went dead.

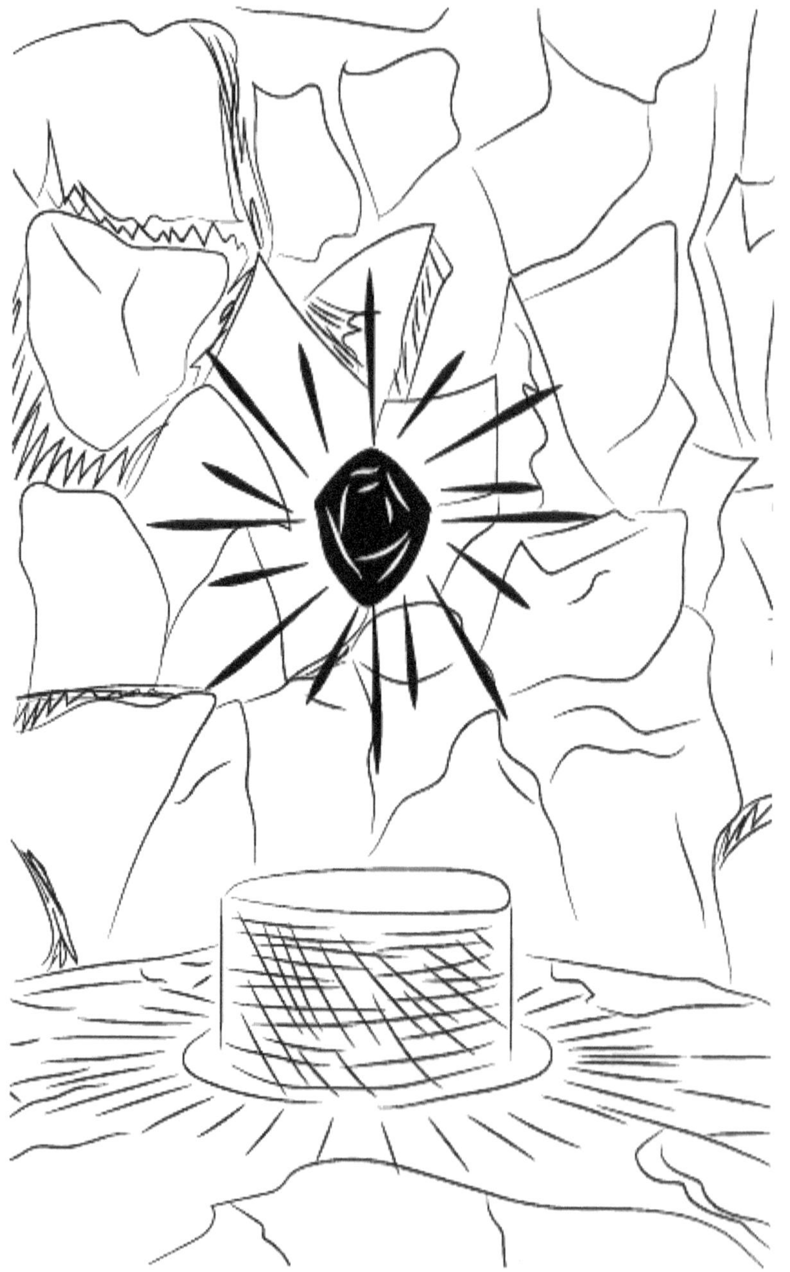

Chapter 7

What the Heart Remembers

Part 1: Shadows Across the Map

The fire in the safehouse had gone out hours ago.

Its last flickers of warmth still curled lazily through the air, but the room had gone cold—quiet, except for the soft, rhythmic tick of an antique wall clock and the quiet scrape of paper as Chloe traced the map with her fingers for the fiftieth time.

They had returned from the archive almost at sunset. Thalia had stuffed the scroll into her satchel with a half-smirk, half-prayer, and Chloe had secured the small metal box.

But Gil's voice over the comms had changed everything.

"We found it … But we weren't alone."

And then—nothing. Silence. Static.

No one else had returned yet. No messages. No coordinates. No idea where everyone was.

Not even Luca's usual "we're alive but also probably going to die soon" voice note.

Chloe stood now, arms crossed, staring at the map now pinned to the wall above the fireplace. The shadows danced along the marked locations: Luzern's subterranean rings, the river beneath the chapel bridge, Hans' ciphered markings, and at the very center, a symbol that hadn't been there before—one she hadn't drawn.

A serpent. Coiled, but the tight circle was broken.

"What does *that* mean?" she murmured.

Thalia sat cross-legged by the fireplace, a thick knitted blanket thrown over her shoulders like a cloak. She was peeling the wax off an old candle and rearranging the fragments into the shape of a spiral.

"It means something's snapped," she said softly. "The coil broke."

Chloe turned. "And what happens when you break something that's been coiled too tightly?"

"You release it?" Thalia said.

Chloe pressed her lips together.

Lily emerged from the back room then, hair damp from the shower, wrapped in a thick wool cardigan several sizes too big. She looked less like a young sleuth and more like a grumpy elf on sick leave.

"No word?" she asked.

Chloe shook her head.

Lily sighed and flopped onto the couch beside Thalia. "I hate this part. The waiting. The not-knowing. It's like being trapped in a horror movie with good lighting."

Thalia offered her a wax fragment. Lily blinked, then took it and started pressing it between her palms.

They waited.

And then, finally, the front lock clicked.

Chloe had her knife out before she realized who it was.

Seraphine slipped inside first, followed by Yuki—mud-streaked, cloak torn, face unreadable. Luca staggered in last, looking as though he'd been run through a washing machine and then kicked by a horse.

"Holy—" Lily shot to her feet. "What happened to you?!"

"We got welcomed by Luzern's unofficial security force," Luca groaned, collapsing into a chair and immediately stealing Thalia's blanket. "Spoiler: they don't like uninvited guests poking around old city tunnels."

Chloe closed the door behind them, scanning their faces. "Where's Gil? Mei? Aoife?"

Seraphine looked at her, and for the first time since Chloe had met her, she looked uncertain.

"We lost contact," she said. "They're somewhere beneath Luzern. They found the chamber. The Heart."

Lily gasped. "They found it?"

Yuki nodded slowly. "Yes. But something was … wrong. They triggered something ancient. Something … watching."

Thalia stood. "Yes, we got a cryptic call from Gil but were cut off. What kind of wrong?"

Seraphine opened her mouth, then closed it again.

Finally, she said, "Before we also lost comms Gil whispered something about there being a figure. Not human. Not exactly."

Chloe felt the air in her lungs freeze.

"The thing Hans hinted at?" she asked. "The thing that was buried?"

"Or guarding," Yuki added.

There was a moment of silence. Then Chloe picked up her notebook and flipped to a clean page.

"Alright," she said. "Let's figure this out. Everything. Start from the beginning."

The Chamber Beneath the Reuss River

They'd found the Heart, suspended mysteriously at the center of the vast chamber.

Then the sound came.

Wet. Dragging. Soft as silk but wrong. The kind of sound that lived like ice in your spine.

They turned as one—and saw the figure in the tunnel. Pale. Watching.

Mei reached for the scanner.

"No," Gil said, pulling her back. "We don't know what it'll trigger."

Aoife stepped forward, lifting her hands slowly.

The figure stepped into the light.

And its face—

No. It *wasn't* a face. Not really.

It was … memory, blurred. Like someone had tried to sculpt a face from fog and failed. The eyes were hollows of shimmering grey. The skin had no pores. And when it moved, it did so without actual movement—like mist reassembling itself into human shape.

It raised one hand.

Gil raised his.

And in the space between them, the Heart pulsed again—and this time, something in the stone beneath them gave a crack.

The light flickered.

The star map vanished.

The figure shimmered in the stuttering light, becoming even more transparent, and smiled slightly.

And the chamber went dark.

Back in the safehouse, Chloe slammed her notebook shut.

"We have to find them."

"Tomorrow," Seraphine said firmly. "Tonight, we rest. Regroup. We need to think—strategically—or we'll all vanish under Luzerne and no one will know what happened."

"But they're out there," Lily protested. "What if—"

"They're trained," Yuki said. "And smart. And they have Aoife. If anyone can sense the way out of that place, it's her."

Chloe sat down slowly. The weight of leadership sat heavier tonight.

Thalia spoke up, soft but clear. "The Heart is a key."

Everyone turned.

"Hans said it anchors Switzerland's neutrality. But neutrality is just *stillness*. Balance. The Heart isn't meant to be used. It's meant to be *guarded*."

Yuki's eyes narrowed. "And it's just been unlocked."

Chapter 8

The Mountain Whispers

The wind hadn't stopped all night.

By morning, snow was knee-deep outside the lodge, and trees bowed beneath the weight of it. The sky was a dull silver, clouds thick and wind whipping. It was the kind of morning that felt stuck in a whirlpool of time—chaotic, confused, and somehow wrong.

Inside the safehouse, the fire hissed in the hearth. Around the old wooden table, the team gathered.

But not everyone was there.

Chloe stood at the frosted window, arms folded tight. Her eyes scanned the tree line.

"Still nothing," she said without turning.

Lily sat on the couch armrest, chewing her thumbnail. "They should've been back hours ago."

"They left before sunrise yesterday," Thalia added, pacing. "They said they'd return by nightfall."

Seraphine sharpened a blade, her hands quicker than usual. "If they got caught in the storm, maybe they took shelter."

"Or something took them," Luca muttered.

Chloe shot him a look, but it lacked heat. Worry haunted all their faces.

"They're smart," Mei said. "Gil's trained. Aoife's strong. Mei's a genius. They'd be prepared."

"I know," Chloe murmured. "It's not them I'm worried about."

The room fell silent. Only the fire's pop and wind's groan filled the space.

Two boxes sat between them. Locked. Ancient. Silent.

Mei traced a symbol on one. "Not normal metal. Altered chemically. Or structurally. Possibly both."

Luca slumped into a chair. "Two creepy boxes. Zero keys. One missing team. Great. Also—starving."

"Luca," Chloe warned.

"What? I get hungry when I'm nervous."

Thalia smirked. "Maybe the third box comes with pancakes and a warning label."

Chloe placed her hands on the pinned map. Her eyes locked on the third marking—high in the range, drawn like a scar.

"That's where they went."

"If they don't come back soon," Lily said, "we go after them."

The wind outside howled louder.

Then—BOOM.

The front door slammed open with a violent gust of snow.

Three figures stumbled inside.

Chloe's heart leapt. "What the—?!"

The storm raged behind them, snow swirling like angry spirits. Gil was in front, face scraped and pale. Mei followed, nearly collapsing as she stumbled inside. Aoife brought up the rear, covered in frost, lips trembling as she forced the door shut.

"Gil!" Chloe rushed to him. "Where were you?!"

He didn't answer. He yanked off his soaked gloves and dropped to the fireplace.

Mei ripped off her goggles, hands shaking.

Aoife's voice cracked. "We went through. Below. Into an old shaft."

Lily moved toward her. "Wait—what shaft?"

"Military-grade," Gil said. "Buried under the western ridge. Hidden. Not on any maps."

"Someone buried it?" Thalia asked.

Mei nodded. "Old. But … active. Someone's been there."

Gil met Chloe's gaze. "We followed a corridor. Cold. Sloped down. It led to under the Reuss River. The deeper we went, the weirder it got. The walls … pulsed."

"Like a machine?" Luca asked, unnerved.

Aoife shook her head. "Like a heartbeat."

Everyone stilled.

"We didn't reach the end," Gil said. "Something was already there."

Mei gripped a thermos from Seraphine and drank. "Not human. Tall. Shadowy. Like … it was made of mist."

"It saw us," Aoife whispered. "Didn't speak. Just … watched."

Chloe felt a chill. "Then what?"

"Vanished," Gil said. "Shimmered and melted into the rock. And then everything went dark. But the cave—it's alive. Something's guarding it."

No one spoke. The fire cracked.

"The boxes," Lily murmured. "Gil we found two boxes, but they're locked, no keys. They're connected, aren't they?"

Gil nodded. "Probably. And part of something bigger. Something that doesn't want to stay hidden. But needs to be protected from people like The Society."

Luca leaned back. "Two boxes, no keys. Maybe the third comes with instructions."

Thalia tapped the map. "The third clue's here then." She tapped an area on the map that was marked with a symbol that looked familiar to her. "This is a Nordic rune, *Algoz*, indicating protection, guardian. But it's further away, deeper. We need to get to Mount Titlis. And we'll need gear … boots with metal cleats. Ice axes."

"I can prep a few things," Yuki said.

Chloe looked around. "We can't stop. These boxes … The Society wants them. Either to recover—or destroy."

Lily nodded. "We're ahead. We stay ahead."

Gil stood. "Then we go. Before another storm hits. Or they do."

The Climb

After a bus ride to Engelberg, the team got a cable car connection to the slopes of Mount Titlis, famous for its ice caves. The climb from there was brutal.

The wind howled. Ice cracked underfoot. The world blurred into a storm of white. Every step forward was a battle.

They moved in silence, breath freezing in the air.

By late afternoon, they found it—a narrow opening in the cliff face, just wide enough for one at a time. Ice shimmered around it, faintly glowing, unnatural.

Thalia stepped through first. "It's … warmer inside."

The passage twisted, tight and dripping. Water echoed from the ceiling.

Then—light.

A vast cavern of blue ice. Walls like diamonds. Pillars rose like frozen gods.

At the center: a pedestal. No symbols. Just a single, small key.

"Is that—?" Lily asked.

"I think it is," Chloe said. "But which box?"

Gil lifted it. No traps. Just silence.

They returned before nightfall.

Chloe placed the key between the two boxes.

Everyone stared.

The key was small. Silver. Cold to the touch.

Chloe turned it over in her hands, then slowly brought it to the first box. Everyone leaned in, holding their breath.

The key slid in smoothly.

Click.

A soft hiss escaped the box as if it had been holding its breath for centuries. The lid creaked open, revealing secrets long buried.

Inside were three items: A folded parchment, a coin covered in strange etchings, and a clear crystal shard that pulsed with soft white light.

Thalia reached forward, her hands steady. She unfolded the parchment gently. "It's a cipher," she murmured. "A mix of Latin, Hebrew, and something even older, maybe Phoenician. And … something unknown. Alien."

Yuki studied the coin, holding it close to the crystal. "It's magnetic," she said, tilting her head. "But not like any magnetic field I've measured. It's reacting to the crystal."

Gil touched the shard. "It's warm," he said, surprised. "Like it's alive."

Chloe's eyes were glued to the items. "This was hidden for a reason. Someone didn't want it found easily."

Luca leaned closer, tapping the base of the box. "Wait. There's a second compartment."

With a click, a small drawer popped open. Inside was a photograph—faded, curling at the edges.

A group of people stood outside a stone building. One man at the front looked far too familiar.

"Is that … Arthur?" Lily breathed.

"Not just him," Aoife said slowly. She pointed to the background. "That symbol—it's the serpent and the sun. The same one from the chamber."

Yuki scanned the photo into her tablet. "This building might still exist. If we find it, we might find the next box. Or a new clue."

Thalia tapped the cipher. "We crack this first. Then we move."

They worked through the night—translating, arguing, scribbling notes.

By dawn, the message was clear: Three keys. Three boxes. One truth buried beneath the oldest ice. A destination: Guttannen.

And a single name: Cassian.

Chloe leaned back, blinking sleep from her eyes. "He's real," she said. "Whoever Cassian is—he was here before us. Maybe he's still ahead of us."

Gil stared at the photo. "Then we're not just chasing The Society. We're searching for *why* whoever hid all this. Whatever it is."

Chapter 9

The Glacier's Memory

Guttannen and the Whispering Mountain

They arrived just as the storm was leaving.

Snow clung to the trees in soft heaps. Wind scattered powder like stardust. The sun, veiled by clouds, cast pale light over jagged ridges.

Guttannen looked carved from the mountains themselves.

It wasn't on their maps.

Not really.

They'd followed coordinates inked on an old Cold War map, flying blind through mountain teeth and wind tunnels. Hans had arranged a friend in the Swiss Guard to fly them by helicopter to the remote mountain village of Guttannen, saying in his rather cryptic note, "Friedrich is an experienced pilot and on our side, he'll get you to your next destination. The secrets waiting there are key for your mission—you'll find friends waiting, Greta, and someone even more closely linked to the Enigma than you'd imagine. She's not just a crack shot and hot pilot either."

Just when Chloe thought they'd turn back, the chopper dipped—descending fast.

She was already there.

Standing alone on the snow-draped clearing—boots buried in the loose snow, scarf whipping in the wind. One gloved hand lifted in greeting.

As the rotors stilled, the team stepped out into brightness.

Elliotte strode forward with mountain-born confidence. Her eyes—smoky-grey and steady—studied them like old puzzle pieces.

"You must be the ones chasing ghosts," she said. "I'm Elliotte Rémy."

"You knew we were coming?" Gil asked.

"Greta sent word. And this mountain's been waiting."

She guided them across the flat clearing—once a helipad, now buried under snow.

"*Bienvenue à l'endroit où le monde oublie de breathe*," Elliotte said. "Welcome to the place where the world forgets to breathe."

Chloe pulled her coat tight. "I assume we were flying low to dodge radar?"

Elliotte smirked. "That too. Mostly to avoid *them*." She nodded toward the mountains.

Gil tensed. "Them who?"

"You'll see."

The village was silent. Wooden houses leaned together like gossiping elders. Smoke curled from chimneys. Goat bells echoed faintly from the slopes.

They passed a faded wooden sign:

Hier schlafen die Götter.

Here, the gods sleep.

Inside a quaint inn, they met Greta—braided, broad, silent. She served hot elderflower tea without a word.

Elliotte said something to her in Swiss-German. Greta nodded once and vanished behind a curtain.

"She knows the stories," Elliotte said. "She grew up with them. So did I."

"Stories like what?" Lily asked.

"The whispering mountain. Men who went missing. Eyes in the ice."

Lily paled. "Please tell me that's metaphor."

"It's not."

Greta returned with a bundle wrapped in thick linen. She placed it on the table with reverence.

Inside: a map.

Hand-drawn. Water-blotched. But clear.

"Military," Yuki said. "Pre-digital. Cold War era."

Elliotte nodded. "Not recorded anywhere official. It wasn't meant to be."

Lines marked tunnels. Bunkers. And one ominous marking beneath a glacier—red ink spelling a single word:

Eisfluch.

Ice Curse.

Aoife touched a pressure line. "There's something under this glacier. A cavity."

"And it's growing," Elliotte said. "Shifting. The ice is cracking."

"The Air Force flew over last year," she added. "Instruments failed. I was the only one who made it back."

"What's down there?" Seraphine asked.

Elliotte's voice dropped. "They call it the Voice. It sleeps. Older than the Alps. Older than memory."

She met each of their eyes.

"And it's starting to wake up. Come, I'll take you to a lodge just outside the village. We've set it up for you as a base of operations."

The Riddle

The glacier was quieter the next morning.

Not still. Never still. But quieter, like it had whispered something in the night and now waited for someone to answer.

The team met Elliotte at Greta's inn, fire crackling high in the hearth, thick mugs of hot chocolate on the table. None of them drank. Not yet.

They gathered around the ancient map, the photo, and Elliotte's military-grade encrypted tablet.

"Let's start with the riddle again," Chloe said.

She unwrapped the parchment, smoothed it out, and read aloud:

"Speak the name of stillness deep. Call the eye that does not sleep. Balance held in frozen breath— Silence binds the dream from death." Above it stood a frozen figure.

Thalia leaned forward. "It's not a riddle. It's a lock," she said. "The words are the key."

Mei nodded slowly. "It's a containment spell. Not to trap, but to lull. To keep something asleep."

Yuki's fingers flew across her keyboard. "I compared the runes from the chamber with seismic glyphs—symbols from early cultures who knew about earthquakes. They match modern fault line patterns. And there's a spiral pattern here."

Luca frowned. "Tell me you didn't just compare ancient magic to earthquakes."

"Oh, I did," Yuki said. "The glacier sits on a fault line. But it hasn't been active in thousands of years."

Aoife inhaled sharply. "Because the Heart anchored it."

"And The Society disturbed one," Gil said. "They shattered a seal."

"They didn't just disturb it," Chloe whispered. "They *wanted* to wake it."

A heavy silence fell.

Seraphine stood, pointing at a photo pinned to the wall. "This rune—here on the figure's chest. It wasn't part of the original design."

Yuki zoomed in. "It's recent. It's been carved into the ice from the inside."

Lily gasped. "It looks like …"

"… The Society's crest," Gil said, his voice like stone.

But it wasn't a simple ouroboros. The serpent was pierced.

Wounded.

And angry.

The Spiral Beneath

By midday, they had mapped the spiral Yuki had uncovered. Seismic clusters. Glacial layers. Historical anomalies.

"It's not random," Yuki said. "It's designed."

She turned her laptop around.

"The Society has been marking the glacier for centuries. The ice has memory—it keeps everything. They've been writing messages in it."

"Messages and instructions," Thalia added. "A language of power."

"There's one more cluster," Gil said, tapping the screen. "South ridge. No one's surveyed it in years."

"Then we go," Elliotte said.

The Sky Turns Dark

They flew out before noon.

Elliotte's unmarked aircraft, sleek and fast, hugged the clouds like a hawk. Everyone wore parachutes—standard, Elliotte claimed. "Just in case."

Luca didn't look convinced.

The ridges grew sharper below. The clouds darker.

Then—

"Two signals," Yuki said, eyes locked on her screen. "No ID. No transponders."

Elliotte cursed. "Hold tight."

Two black helicopters emerged from the clouds like phantoms. Fast. Silent.

Doors slid open.

"They're mercs," Seraphine said. "Society hitmen."

Gunfire shredded the silence.

"Straps on!" Chloe shouted.

Sparks flew as bullets grazed the fuselage. One helicopter dropped a grappling drone.

"They're boarding!" Yuki yelled.

Gil charged toward the door as it opened, crowbar in hand. A masked figure pulled himself through.

Gil swung. The figure fell.

But wind rushed in—

And Lily, too close to the opening, lost her footing, slid as the aircraft banked sharply.

"LILY!" Chloe screamed.

A flash of red parachute.

Then—gone.

Gil caught Chloe before she jumped after her. "She knows what to do. She'll land. She's trained."

"She's my sister!" Chloe sobbed.

"She's Sisterhood," Gil said. "She'll survive."

The Society choppers wheeled off, their attempt at boarding foiled. Elliotte banked the aircraft, now trailing smoke. "We're going after her."

Into the White

The world below was a blur of snow and shadow.

A single red parachute floated far beneath.

The mountain waited.

So did the truth.

Chapter 10

Secrets Frozen in the Stone

Part 1: Swallowed by the Mountain

The fall was longer than it should've been. Not in seconds—but in feeling. The air screamed past Lily's ears, tearing at her coat and hair. Her gloves fumbled at the strap on her chest. Her brain told her to panic.

But her training kicked in.

She yanked the parachute chord.

The chute opened with a loud crack. Her body jolted, jerking painfully as the harness caught. The white world slowed. Snow swirled below. Wind roared above.

And then she saw it.

A crack in the mountain.

No—worse. A mouth gaped.

Darkness waited, wide and round, where the mountain split like lips.

The wind shifted. The chute tilted. Lily screamed—but it was swallowed by the cold.

She was pulled downward. Into the mouth of the mountain.

There was no more sky. Only the fall. And then—impact.

The Hollow Ice

Lily landed hard.

Not on sharp rock. Not on soft snow.

But on something strange. Cold, but not hard. Spongy, like frozen foam. Her shoulder screamed. Her hip throbbed. Her lungs burned.

She rolled onto her side and groaned. The parachute tangled above her like torn wings.

Above, the hole in the glacier was vanishing, obscured by the falling snow.

She was alone.

She unzipped her emergency pouch. Flashlight. Knife. Thermos. Signal flare. A small compass that spun wildly.

She clicked the flashlight on. The beam struck the wall—and bounced back with a shimmer.

She was inside a tunnel. A perfect circle. Carved. Not natural.

The walls were blue ice streaked with silver and gold. Not painted. Not added. Grown.

Symbolic writing coiled across the walls like frost. Some pulsed. Like breathing.

Lily's breath caught.

The tunnel stretched ahead in both directions. Dark. Silent. Waiting.

She chose the right. And walked.

The First Signs

Lily counted her steps. It helped keep her calm.

She passed a curved bend—and the tunnel opened into a wider chamber. The walls changed. Darker. Lined with veins of red and gold.

She swept her flashlight slowly.

There it was.

A symbol. Burned into the ice. A spiral. Glowing.

And beside it—

Footprints. Bare. Too long. Too narrow.

Not human. Not old.

Lily swallowed.

"Okay," she whispered. "This is fine. Creepy. But fine."

And she moved on.

Above: The Team Lands

Elliotte's jet landed hard, skidding across a snow basin, sending up clouds of white.

They were down. But the aircraft wouldn't fly again.

No one waited. No one rested.

"Parachute—half a click east!" Elliotte called. "She's down. Somewhere deep."

"Can we find her?" Chloe asked, slipping on her gloves.

"The mountain can," Elliotte said. "If it lets her be found."

Gil adjusted his harness. "Let's go—now!"

They set off, fast and focused. Chloe's heart thudded like war drums. Lily was out there. And the mountain wasn't done with them yet.

Beneath the Ice: Lily's Discovery

The chamber she entered was warmer. Not by much. But enough.

At its center stood a strange structure. An altar? A spine of ice covered in symbolic writing. Faint handprints marked the surface.

Around the base, carvings: Figures curled in pain. Others reaching upward.

And one—a woman. Hair like flame. Eyes closed. Arms raised.

Above her—a frozen figure. Like on the parchment. But here—it smiled.

Lily stumbled backward. Her foot crunched something.

She looked down.

A skull.

Human.

She turned and ran.

The shadows behind her moved.

She didn't see them.

Not yet.

Part 2: Going Below

The mountain hummed.

Not noise. But pressure.

As the team approached the chasm, they felt it—

a vibration. A rhythm.

The torn parachute flapped weakly on a jagged piece of ice surrounding a gaping hole.

"This hole—it's not natural," Aoife whispered. "Cut. Then frozen again."

"Can we follow her?" Chloe asked.

"We have to," Gil said.

He and Elliotte secured ropes and dropped them. They began the descent.

The deeper they went, the more the mountain whispered.

Lily's Tunnel

The passages twisted.

The ice grew darker.

Lily's torch flickered.

She smacked it. It stayed on.

And then—

Movement.

She turned. Nothing. But her skin tingled.

A breath.

Too close.

She ran.

Turned left. Then right.

Straight into a wall.

Solid.

Where a tunnel had been.

Her flashlight died.

Dark.

And in the dark: A voice. Not sound. But emotion. Sad. Hungry.

It filled her head.

She crouched down and waited.

The Team Splits

They landed in a wide chamber. Runes lit the walls faintly.

Yuki checked her tablet. "One lifeform. Close."

"Could be Lily," Chloe said.

"Or a trap," Seraphine added.

"We'll find out."

Chloe, Gil, and Elliotte headed down the left path. Aoife, Thalia, and Yuki took the right.

The others stayed to guard the entrance.

The air thickened. The walls pulsed.

The glacier was waking.

Chloe, Gil, Elliotte

They found a message, scratched in the ice on the floor:

She was chosen.

Chloe touched it.

"What does it mean?"

Elliotte's hand reached for the wall. The ice responded.

It moved.

Glowed. Sang. An ethereal sound almost beyond hearing

Her skin lit up—pale blue. Like the symbolic writing on the walls.

"I didn't remember," she said. "Until the voice started singing."

Aoife, Thalia, Yuki

The tunnel erupted ahead.

Two masked figures emerged, guns drawn.

"Down!" Yuki yelled.

Aoife flicked her knife in a deadly accurate arc.

The first man hit the wall, grabbing his leg, falling to the ground.

Thalia whispered something in Gaelic, something ancient.

The second dropped.

Unmoving.

Yuki stared.

"What did you say?"

Thalia shivered.

"A curse. From my grandmother. I didn't believe it worked. Something about this place must have given it power."

They turned and ran towards voices—Lily's voice, and Chloe's.

Lily

She saw scratched symbolic writing in the wall. The ones Chloe had studied.

"Balance. Silence. Stillness. Dream."

As she read them out aloud, the wall cracked.

Light.

A figure shimmered in the ice. Cloaked.

"You and your team are not ready … yet," the woman said.

And vanished.

The wall suddenly melted away without a sound, leaving a shallow pool of water in its wake that quickly iced over.

Chloe appeared.

"Lily!"

She ran to her sister.

But they weren't alone. Society agents flooded in, led by a woman in grey. She looked like a Gestapo commander, with closely cropped hair and a rigid military stance.

"You shouldn't have come," she barked.

The glacier trembled.

Elliotte glowed brighter.

She raised her hand.

The ice answered.

And the mountain shook.

Part 3: The Voice Beneath

The woman in grey stared at Elliotte.

"So, *you* are the last of the Mountain Watch."

Elliotte stepped forward. "I was born here," she said. "I belong to the ice."

Her skin pulsed, lighting up with blue and silver symbols..

The same symbolic writing in the walls lit up.

Elliotte sang a long clear note, echoing off the walls.

The Society agents raised their weapons … but they couldn't fire.

The mountain flung them back with a powerful blast of icy frost, slamming them to the ground.

The woman hissed as she clambered back to her feet, "You can't stop us."

"I was born to stop you," Elliotte replied.

The Collapse

"Seismic spike!" Yuki yelled as she and the rest of the team arrived. "It's falling apart!"

"Run!" Seraphine ordered.

The glacier groaned.

Chloe grabbed Lily. Gil pulled Elliotte.

The ceiling cracked.

Yuki fired a flare.

Its red glow lit up—

A second face.

In the wall.
Smiling.

The Escape

They ran. Sliding. Ducking falling ice.

Aoife shouted directions. "Left! Up! Now!"

They reached a gate … not a door.

An archway, covered in runes and strange writing.
It pulsed.

A pedestal stood before it.
Empty.

Gil froze. "This held something."

"A Heart," Mei whispered.

Elliotte touched it.

The mountain sang.

A tunnel of blinding white light opened.

"Where does it go?" Lily asked.

"To what comes next," Elliotte said.

The glacier cracked behind them.

Chloe shoved Lily through the gate.

One by one, they leapt through.

And the gate vanished.

In the silence left in chamber, the cloaked woman knelt by the altar.

She touched it, nodding.

"She is marked," she whispered.

Behind her, a frozen figure opened its eyes.

And smiled.

Erinnert euch,

was ihr

vergessen

habt.

Chapter 11

Through the Gates

The world reassembled itself in silence. No light. No sky. No falling ice. Just breath—slow, cold, damp, and ancient.

When Chloe opened her eyes, the first thing she saw was stone. Smooth, dark stone. It gleamed blue-black like wet obsidian, polished by centuries of memory. She was lying on it, her chest heaving, her heart thumping like a hammer.

One by one, the others stirred.

Lily was beside her, curled in on herself like a cat, her hair stuck to her cheeks. Gil was glancing at Chloe, then climbing to his feet to stand at the edge of the vast stone platform, eyes scanning the darkness, his shoulders tense. Elliotte was still, sprawled near the center, her limbs tangled. Chloe scrambled toward her, terrified—until Elliotte's fingers twitched.

Alive.

Aoife, Mei, Yuki, Thalia, Luca, and Seraphine were scattered across the platform like leaves after a windstorm. Each groaned and blinked as they took in the space around them.

But it wasn't the landing that made their skin prickle. It was the silence. Not empty. Not peaceful. But full—too full. It buzzed just under the surface. A hum. A whisper. Like voices just beyond hearing.

"This place …" Thalia murmured. "It's listening."

And it was.

Another Gate

They stood slowly, brushing off ice-melt and small chunks of glacier.

The air was cold, but not bitterly so. The chamber they stood in stretched outwards in all directions— massive, ancient, carved right into the mountain's heart. The walls sparkled faintly, laced with silver and copper lines that pulsed when someone breathed too close.

There were no lights. Yet the room glowed.

"It's like being inside a gem," Lily said softly. She pressed her hand to the floor. "Hey, it's kinda warm."

"No torches. No tech. And yet ..." Yuki knelt beside her. "This place is alive."

Aoife stepped carefully, her boots quiet. "This isn't a building. It's a vault.."

At the far end of the hall stood another gate. Not a normal gate. Not metal. Not stone. Not anything they'd ever seen.

It shimmered like oil on water—layers of color that changed as you looked at it. It breathed. Moved. Waited.

Above it, carved deep into the arch of ice surrounding it:

Einrest euch was iht vergessen habt. Remember what you forgot.

Elliotte frowned, her eyes locked on the words. "I've been here before."

Gil blinked. "You said you were born in Guttannen."

"I was," she said. "But I remember this place. I was brought here as a child."

Chloe frowned. "Why?"

Elliotte stared at the gate.

"They told me I was a Watcher."

Whispers

Having passed through the shimmering gate, the further they walked, the stranger it became.

The walls murmured.

Not in voices they recognized. But voices from memories—some long buried, some raw, fresh. Chloe stopped at one point and heard her own voice echo softly:

"I can't lose her again."

She turned. No one had spoken.

Luca froze by a carved alcove. "I heard my mother," he whispered. "She used to sing that song."

"But she died ten years ago," Yuki said.

"I know."

Thalia pressed her fingers to the stone. "It's not just memory. It's … reflection. This place holds thoughts."

"Or it's trying to understand us," Aoife added. "Like we're the ones being studied."

The Hall of Names

They followed a spiral staircase down into a new chamber. Deeper. It felt older.

Here, the walls were covered with names.

Names in all languages, carved into the stone, layered like scales on a dragon's skin. Millions upon millions of names.

Some glowed gold. Some pulsed red.

"It's a record," Seraphine said. "A living one."

Yuki gasped. "These … these are Society codenames. Hidden files. Classified names. How does this place know them?"

"It knows everything," Mei said quietly. "Past. Present. Future."

Gil pointed. "Look. That name hasn't been born yet, it's still forming."

And that was when the chaos started.

The Breach

It started with a metallic whine. Then light. Harsh, artificial light.

A hole tore through the ceiling.

A drone dropped through—sleek and humming.

Then two black-clad Society operatives descended on ropes.

"Down!" Gil shouted.

Seraphine moved like lightning, dropping one with a single shot.

Luca tossed a magnetic grenade that fried the drone.

Chloe grabbed Lily's hand.

A second shot rang out.

Gil dropped to one knee, clutching his leg.

"Gil!" Chloe cried, running to him.

"Go!" he grunted. "Don't stop!"

But Elliotte stood frozen.

Then she screamed.

Elliotte's Memory Comes Alive

The second operative leveled a weapon at Chloe.

Elliotte stepped in front.

A sound burst from her—a note, high and pure.

The walls pulsed. The writing on them flared. Elliotte glowed.

The operative fell, clutching his ears, eyes wide.

Chloe stared. "What did you do?"

Elliotte's face was pale. "I remembered."

"Remembered what?"

"That I wasn't just born near the mountain." She turned slowly toward the gate. "I was meant to protect it, keep it asleep."

A Sacrifice?

They fled to a side tunnel, Gil leaning on Mei.

But someone was missing.

"Aoife," Chloe breathed. "Where is she?"

Seraphine's face fell. "She was behind me. She was covering us."

"No …"

They turned back, but the tunnel behind them began to fall.

Through the falling dusty ice they could see Aoife, she stood alone.

She smiled. Then slammed her staff into the floor.

The ceiling collapsed.

Cutting her off.

The Gate of Voices

The others ran.

Twisting passages. Heat rising.

Then—another chamber.

A new gate. Smaller. Covered in different runes.

A pedestal before it.

Empty.

Gil stumbled to it. "This was also made for the Heart. Or *a* Heart"

"Yes," Mei said. "A third."

Elliotte stepped forward and touched the stone.

It sang.

The gate shimmered.

Writing appeared above it.

Der Stimmen Bleiben. The voices remain.

A corridor of white light opened behind it.

"Where does it go?" Lily asked.

Elliotte met her eyes. "To the truth."

The Chase

They heard boots behind them.

Society agents.

One raised a rifle.

"Now!" Chloe yelled.

She shoved Lily through the gate.

Gil followed.

One by one, they jumped.

Chloe was last.

And the gate closed.

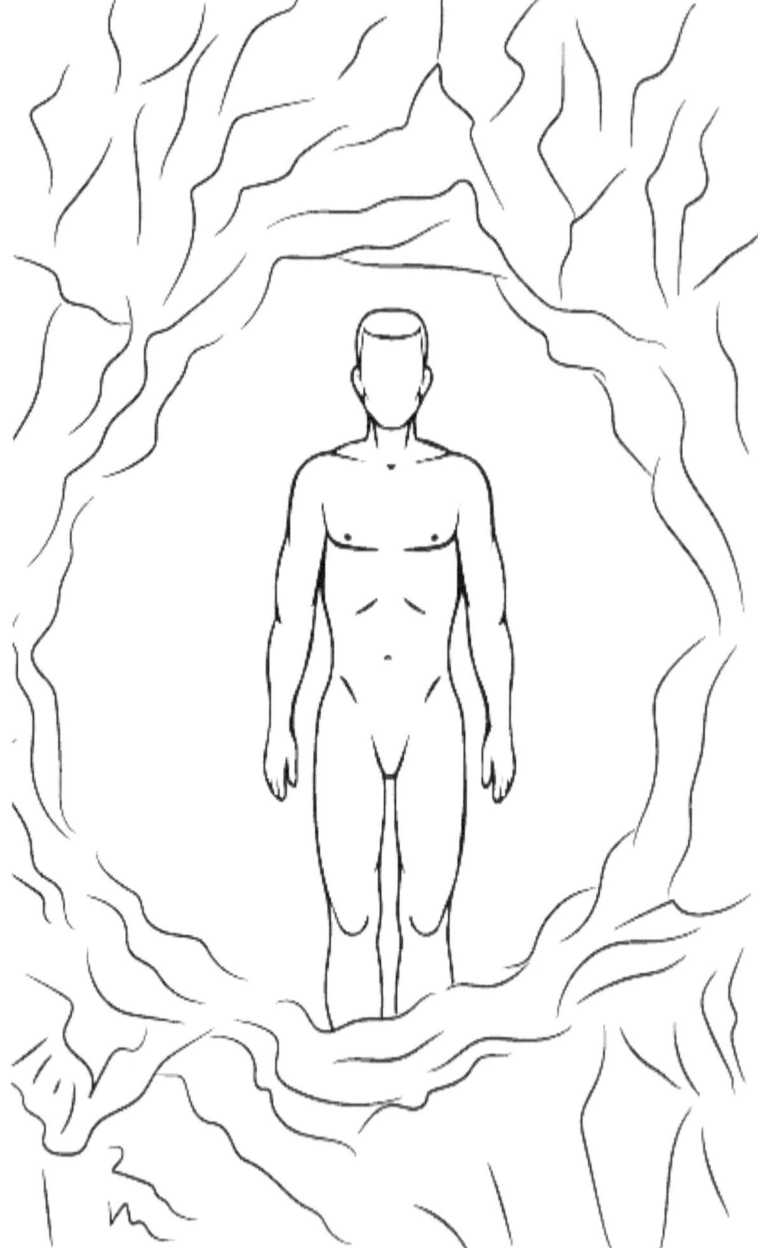

Chapter 12

The Dream That Listens

Once through the gate, they were presented with another staircase—the steps descended for what felt like forever, twisting in different directions every now and then.

Each footstep echoed softly, swallowed by the dark. The air grew warmer as they went deeper, strangely warm for being under a frozen mountain. It wasn't just heat. It felt alive—damp, heavy, and thick, like the slow breath of something enormous sleeping below.

"Are we almost there?" Lily whispered, clutching her flashlight tighter.

"Almost," Gil answered, his voice strained. He was still limping from the wound on his leg, but he kept moving, leaning on Mei now and then when the pain got too strong. No one had the heart to tell him to stop.

The staircase twisted one final time—and then ended.

They stepped into a vast chamber, and everyone froze.

It was like nothing they had ever seen.

Their flashlights, flickering and weak, were hardly needed. The room glowed faintly on its own, as if the very walls remembered the sun. The light wasn't bright, but soft—like dawn peeking through curtains, or moonlight on still water.

Tall columns rose from the stone floor to the curved roof far above, each one carved with symbolic phrases and images from another age. Moss and silver fungi clung to the edges, glowing faintly with a bluish tint. In the very center of the room was a raised round platform, surrounded by a shallow ring of water.

And on the platform: a pedestal.

Empty.

"This feels like a temple," Mei whispered. Her voice barely carried, but it felt wrong to speak louder.

Yuki stepped beside her, scanning the walls with her device. Her eyebrows knit together. "There's energy flowing here. Not electricity—something deeper. It's moving through the stone, like veins flowing with blood under skin."

Chloe slowly stepped forward. Her eyes never left the pedestal.

"Something used to be here," she said quietly.

Gil, still alert despite the pain, swept his flashlight toward the shadows between the pillars. "Or maybe it still is."

They moved slowly around the room, careful not to disturb the silence. The walls were covered with old carvings—scenes of people kneeling before the pedestal, offering strange objects. Books. Crystals. Scrolls. Each gift held out to a tall, featureless figure with no face.

"Same symbol again," Lily pointed out, touching a part of the wall where a carving showed the serpent coiled tightly around the sun.

"They've used it everywhere," Luca muttered. He crouched at the edge of the water, dipped his fingers in. "It's warm. Not deep. Might be geothermal?"

"No," Aoife said quietly. She stood with her arms folded, staring hard at the rippling pool. "It's not natural."

Before anyone could respond, a low hum vibrated through the chamber.

The water trembled.

Yuki gasped and dropped her scanner. "Something's coming online."

Around the edge of the chamber, a ring of symbols suddenly flared to life—glowing softly, one by one, in a slow-moving circle. Like stars waking.

Seraphine lifted her crossbow at once. "Whatever this is … we've activated it."

A click echoed from the center of the platform. The pedestal moved.

A small, hidden compartment slid open.

Inside was a glowing blue shard—just like the one from the first box.

It pulsed gently, as though waiting.

Chloe stepped forward without thinking. Her breath caught in her throat. She reached out—

And touched it.

In an instant, a flood of images crashed behind her eyes.

Mountains collapsing. Dark figures in long coats watching from cliffs. A hand holding three shards—

light exploding from the center like a newborn star. And then … darkness.

She stumbled back, her hand shaking.

Gil caught her before she could fall. "Are you alright?"

"I think … I think we just woke something up," she said. Her voice trembled.

Yuki picked up the shard carefully and held it under her scanner. "It's not just a key. It's part of something alive. Something ancient."

"Then we need to figure out what it's trying to say," Mei said, stepping forward. "Before The Society gets here."

They moved on into a smaller chamber beyond the glowing circle. It was quieter here. More peaceful. Almost like a sanctuary.

The walls were covered in more symbolic lettering—layers upon layers of symbols, so many that they twisted over one another in places. Looking at them too long made Chloe's head spin.

The light didn't come from torches or lanterns. It came from the stone itself, which pulsed softly with a rhythm—like breathing.

Gil sat down heavily, leaning against one of the carved columns. Mei was already kneeling beside him, working fast.

"You're lucky it didn't hit an artery," she said, cleaning his wound with warm snow water from her flask, dressing it with supplies from her medical kit. "You'd be dead."

Gil gave her a weak smile. "Wouldn't be the first time luck had excellent timing."

Thalia sat apart from the group, her fingers tracing the carvings around her. She wasn't talking. But Chloe noticed her eyes. Wide. Bright. Watching, deciphering.

"This place is alive," Yuki said softly. "Not in a way we're used to. Not with cells and muscles. But in resonance. In memory."

Mei joined her, and soon both were busy comparing symbols to musical notes using their devices. Soft beeps and hums filled the air.

"It's a cipher," Mei said. "A song written in stone."

Luca raised an eyebrow. "A song?"

"Each symbolic writing is like a note. Together they create a … sort of … lullaby," Yuki explained.

"No," Thalia said suddenly.

She was kneeling now, near the pedestal where the shard had been.

"Wait, it's not a lullaby," she said, her voice low. "It's a prophecy."

She traced one cluster of symbols carefully. The rest of the group moved closer.

Her fingers stopped on a carved line.

"When the one who listens to stone sings," she read aloud, "the glacier shall bleed."

While they took the opportunity to rest, Elliotte sat alone near the pedestal.

She was quiet, her legs crossed, her hands resting in her lap.

The air around her shimmered faintly. The symbols pulsed with her heartbeat. Her skin still glowed with silvery echoes of the symbols.

When she closed her eyes, the visions came—strange, vivid, and far too real.

She saw women standing at the top of a frozen mountain, holding hands and singing in perfect harmony as one voice. She saw a shape buried beneath the glacier, not a man, not a beast, not a god. Watching.

She saw the Society, hundreds of years ago, finding this place and marking it on a map with blood.

And she saw her mother. Young. Terrified. Carrying a child wrapped in mountain cloth.

"I am the last Watcher," Elliotte whispered. "And this is what they tried to make me forget."

The betrayal came in a cough.

Luca, sitting near the back, suddenly doubled over, hacking violently. Mei rushed to help him—but when she reached him, she froze.

His comm unit was glowing.

"Yuki," Mei called.

Yuki hurried over, eyes narrowing.

"Who are you trying to contact? And why so secretive?"

Chloe drew her dagger slowly. "Luca … what are you not telling us?"

He looked up, guilt written across his face.

"They blackmailed me. Months ago. My brother disappeared in Prague. They said if I just left … breadcrumbs, they'd return him. Cast doubt. Not locations. Just little clues to throw you off."

There was an assortment of reactions from each of them, a gasp, a sigh, a snort. Gil shook his head and groaned.

Seraphine stepped forward, glowering, crossbow low but ready. "And you believed them?"

"I hoped," he whispered. He smashed the comm unit against the wall. It shattered.

"I know better now."

Mei shook her head. "Why didn't you just tell us? We could've helped figure out a way to stymie them?"

Luca didn't answer, just sat dejectedly looking at his hands, then the pieces of broken comm unit.

Chloe studied him for a long moment. "We'll get your brother back. Or Arthur can arrange to look for him. But Luca—no more lies. Not down here."

She turned to the others.

"We vote."

It wasn't unanimous.

Yuki wanted to seal the chamber.

Mei wanted to study it.

Seraphine wanted to destroy it.

But Elliotte stood firm.

"It's not evil," she said. "It's change. The Society wants to turn it into a weapon. We have to understand it first."

Gil looked at Chloe. His face was pale, but his voice was steady. "What's your call?"

Chloe took a deep breath. She felt the mountain beneath her feet tremble slightly—like something waiting.

"We listen first," she said. "Then we choose."

She turned to Elliotte.

"Sing."

The gate didn't open with noise.

It opened with silence.

Elliotte stood tall, her eyes closed, her face calm. And then her voice rose—soft, clear, and pure, weaving through the chamber like a ribbon of light.

The walls began to glow brighter.

Gold.

The air shivered.

And then came the sound.

It wasn't loud. It was deep. Almost subliminal. Ancient. So low it felt like the stone was breathing it. A song older than any language.

The chamber stopped moving.

Even time seemed to pause.

And far below them—beneath the ice and rock—a shadow turned.

Chapter 13

The Power of Sound

The tremor began at the edge of hearing. A low pulse, rhythmic and ancient, like the beat of a heart buried beneath stone and silence. It echoed through the walls of the chamber, subtle at first—the kind of vibration one might dismiss as imagined. But it grew. And with it came the unmistakable sensation of being watched.

The team was exhausted. In the hours since the Gate had opened, time seemed to behave differently. Minutes stretched. Shadows deepened. And something beneath them—beneath the glacier, beneath the mountain—had begun to listen back.

Gil, pale from blood loss but still standing, pressed his palm to the stone. "It's awake."

Chloe exchanged a glance with Elliotte. "No," Elliotte said softly. "It's been awake. It's just … listening now. Fully."

They had gathered back in the circular hall where symbolic lettering still pulsed across the floor and ceiling in slow, golden arcs. The voices had stopped whispering. Now, they hummed. Low. Melodic. Inescapable.

"We can't stay here," Seraphine said. "The resonance is increasing. It could hurt us, fry our brains or damage our eardrums if it peaks."

"Where would you have us go?" Thalia asked. "Outside? Into the arms of The Society?"

"At least The Society bleeds," Seraphine snapped. "I can fight them. I can't fight a mountain that thinks."

Elliotte sat cross-legged near the gate, her eyes closed, lips barely moving. She wasn't asleep. She was listening.

Chloe knelt beside her. "What are you hearing?"

"Images," Elliotte whispered. "Music. Not like ours. It's ... mathematical. Celestial. It remembers before we had mouths to name things."

"Does it want something?"

Elliotte opened her eyes. "It wants us to know."

Yuki and Mei had moved to the glyph chamber, their scanners whirring softly. They spoke in clipped, efficient exchanges, weaving frequency maps and harmonic symbols into a new pattern.

"This is the final piece," Yuki said, pointing to a vibrating line embedded in the stone. "The closing sequence. But …"

"There's a cost," Mei said.

Chloe entered behind them. "What kind of cost?"

"A harmonic exchange," Mei replied. "The gate was opened with balance. To close it, that balance must be restored. A frequency given … and one taken."

"One of us?"

Mei didn't answer.

They held council beside the sleeping gate. Chloe led. Her voice didn't tremble, but the weight behind it grew heavier with every word.

"We have a choice. Communicate with it. Learn what it wants. Or try to seal it before The Society brings it under their control."

"If they haven't already," Seraphine muttered.

Gil stood with Mei and Yuki. Thalia remained unreadable, her hands always busy etching new runes into stone or sketching spirals in dust.

Elliotte said nothing.

It was Lily who finally asked the question none of them wanted to voice. "What if it's not trying to get out? What if it's trying to warn us?"

"Well let's go find out. We go deeper in," Chloe said after a few seconds.

Gil nodded.

The expedition into the deeper beyond then began. Five went: Chloe, Gil, Elliotte, Lily, and Thalia.

The corridor spiraled downward in impossible geometry. The floor bent light. The walls sang. And time bent in strange ways.

They passed through more chambers that replayed ancient visions—wars lost before the first stone city rose, civilizations swallowed by ice, promises made in blood and preserved in ice.

In one chamber, Chloe saw herself—older, hollow-eyed, standing alone in a ruined cathedral.

"This isn't prophecy," Thalia murmured. "It's possibility. Time is malleable."

Elliotte was silent. The song had grown stronger.

They reached the lowest chamber just as the glacier began to bleed. It wasn't blood. But it looked like it—

veins of glowing crimson carving themselves through the ice, pulsing with memory.

At the center stood the being. It was not a god. It was not a monster. It was presence. Vast. Coiled. Shifting between shape and sound.

Elliotte stepped forward. The song rose. And Chloe, for a moment, saw everything. The stars, turning like gears. The Heart breaking. The Society stealing from time. And then she felt herself slipping. Falling into the sound. Losing her mind, her Self, her name—

A hand caught hers. Lily.

"Come back."

The words were soft, but they shattered the vision. Chloe gasped, reeling, and the presence … paused. Acknowledged. And offered its final memory: A city beneath the sea. A symbol: a broken crown, burning. And a word spoken in fire: *Parthenope*.

They returned changed.

Aiofe, sweating and breathless, skidded in to join Mei, Yuki, and Seraphine. "I did what I could to stop them but they're coming – and they've got something big with them. We need to take a stand here, stand fast!"

The Society arrived within minutes of Aiofe's warning—a group of black-clad figures carrying a mechanism they assembled within seconds, efficient and practiced. Others, armed, took up stations around it to protect it.

They made their final move. A weapon: the Anti-Resonance Pulse. An anti-song of silence meant to erase memory, destroy thought, collapse legacy.

Yuki and Mei raced to counter it. Elliotte stepped through and stood before the gate, arms wide.

"You can break the gate," she said. "But not what it guards."

The Pulse fired but Elliotte sang.

And the mountain held.

The Pulse backfired.

The Society's line collapsed—all their agents fell to the ground clutching their heads, screaming in agony. Their future … unwritten.

In the aftermath, Chloe stood once more at the Gate of Voices. It was closing. But not sealed. Elliotte had given enough to restore balance. For now.

They had seen the future. And the real war was not behind them. It waited. Beneath Naples. And the serpent was no longer sleeping.

Chapter 14

And Red Makes Three

The walk back to the surface felt longer. Everyone was quiet, each of them carrying the weight of what they had just seen—and what Chloe had felt. The shard pulsed faintly in her pack, like a heartbeat echoing in stone.

As they walked, Yuki powered up her equipment. "If we're right, each shard is more than just a piece. It's a message. A map. Or maybe … a warning."

Lily hovered beside her. "The visions. They weren't random. They were showing us something. A future? A memory?"

"It could be both," Mei offered. "Sometimes the past and the future feel the same when the danger is big enough. According to quantum theory, all time exists simultaneously. It's very complicated."

"Ouch, just thinking about that makes my head hurt," Lily said, shaking her head.

Gil turned to face Chloe. "We've got to assume The Society is moving. We need to act before they do."

Aoife reached into her pack, took out the map and spread it out again. "If there's a third shard, it has to be somewhere connected to the others. A triangulation point."

Chloe traced her finger along the parchment. "Here. This ridge. Arthur said it was sealed off after an avalanche ten years ago. It hasn't been touched since."

Luca raised an eyebrow. "Avalanche … or cover-up?"

"Let's find out," Thalia said, "it's not too far from here …"

They trudged on. The ridge was as treacherous as it was beautiful. High winds howled across the ledges, and ice snapped beneath their boots. But they pressed on.

Finally, they found it. A buried archway, barely visible beneath a thick wall of ice.

Yuki rigged a small charge—just enough to crack the surface. When the ice fell away, a narrow corridor appeared, hidden behind what had once looked like part of the mountain itself.

Inside, the air was still. Expectant.

They switched their flashlights on and stepped through. The walls here were rougher, carved in haste. The markings were older—jagged, uneven, but unmistakable.

"It's the same language, similar runes," Lily whispered. "But more … desperate."

The tunnel opened into a chamber shaped like a dome. In the center was another pedestal.

And resting on it, the third crystal shard. This one glowed red.

They stepped closer. No traps. No guardians.

"Almost too easy," Seraphine muttered.

Chloe reached out, her hand hovering above the shard. "Everyone ready?"

They nodded.

She touched it.

A flash. This time they all saw it—

Fire. Ash. A city in ruins. Voices crying out. A vault opening. A figure in the distance, cloaked, smiling, soulless eyes.

Then darkness.

They staggered as they were thrown back into the present.

Chloe gripped the shard tightly. "Whatever this is …
it's coming. And we're the only ones who can stop it."

Chapter 15

The Flimsy Walkway
- A Deadly Escape

The ancient alpine atmosphere outside had fallen still. Not in peace. But in that unnatural silence that follows catastrophe—when the world seems to hold its breath in fear of what might come next.

The gate had dimmed. The mountain was no longer singing. Elliotte's voice had repelled the Pulse, and the entity beneath had quieted again. They'd retrieved the third crystal shard. But The Society was not gone.

They still had a long way to get back and no help was coming.. They had no aircraft.

Only feet.

And a long, punishing walk around the frozen peaks of the Swiss Alps.

The air up here was thin. The kind that bit your lungs like ice and turned sweat to frost before it even touched your skin.

Gil led the way, thigh bound from his wound, eyes ever scanning the jagged skyline. They moved in single file across a knife-edge ridge, no one speaking much. Even Luca, normally incapable of silence, said nothing.

Snow had begun to fall again.

Just lightly. Like ash.

And then, after a steep climb that left them breathless and coughing, the trail ended.

Not in a cliff.

But in something worse.

A bridge.

It was swaying, creaking in the wind. A long wooden span suspended between two mountain peaks, its supports nailed into black stone. It looked flimsy, ancient, and looked alarmingly precarious.

Lily swallowed. "No. Nope. I'm not doing that. That is not a bridge. That is a death trap that someone had the audacity to name."

Gil exhaled slowly. "It's our only way forward. The pass is too narrow to double back. The Society will be on us soon."

Aoife ran her hand along one of the frayed ropes anchoring the bridge. It moaned under her fingers.

"This thing is held together by nostalgia and regrets," she said.

Chloe stepped beside Gil. "We don't have a choice. But we go smart. Single file. Light packs."

Seraphine was already checking her weapon, eyes on the horizon. "We won't have long before they find us. If we're going to do this, it has to be now."

Mei knelt beside one of the posts. "I don't like the vibration. Something's off."

Elliotte stared across the ravine. Her lips were pale. The wind tugged her braid like a warning.

"I sense a pressure shift," she said. "They're coming."

And she was right.

Because the shot came a second later.

And the first support beam exploded into splinters.

"Run!" Gil's voice split the air.

The team scattered instinctively, Chloe grabbing Lily's hand and dragging her toward the nearest edge of the bridge. Splinters scattered. A second shot rang out, carving a neat hole through a nearby plank.

Luca pulled his hood tighter as the wind howled. "I am never trusting old wood again!"

Elliotte already had her foot halfway onto the bridge, her boots slipping slightly on the ice-glazed planks. She pulled back. The bridge had creaked alarmingly beneath her slight weight.

"Gil!" Chloe shouted. "We can't all go at once!"

"We won't," he snapped, tossing his pack aside. "I'll go first. Secure a rope."

He sprinted forward, dodging a broken beam, and leapt over a yawning gap in the bridge. His boots landed hard on the other side of a broken segment, the wooden plank bowing under him.

He hooked a climbing line to a support, wound it tight around his waist, and flung the coil back to Chloe.

"One at a time! Use the rope!"

Chloe clipped in first. Followed by Lily.

Breathless and wide-eyed, they each began sliding hand over hand, feet slipping on the slick boards as the bridge groaned again.

Another shot.

This one shattered a post near Luca, sending ropes whipping wildly in the wind.

Seraphine returned fire with icy precision, ducking low, buying time.

Mei and Thalia crossed next.

Then Luca.

Elliotte started, but the beam under her feet split.

She shrieked, arms flailing—

And Luca caught her.

Dangling over the abyss, her braid whipping across her face, Elliotte clung to his wrists.

"Don't you dare drop me!"

"Not unless you plan to fly!"

With a grunt, he hauled her up, both collapsing in a heap on the swaying bridge.

Two agents burst through the ridge behind them.

Chloe screamed, and Seraphine turned just in time, firing two shots that sent the nearest agent staggering.

The other charged.

Elliotte pivoted, kicked loose a rotting board behind her, and the agent fell, arms flailing, into the abyss.

Luca and Elliotte didn't wait to see him land.

They ran.

Across the final boards.

Onto solid stone.

Shaking. Bleeding. Alive.

Aiofe severed the ropes securing the bridge to their end and it fell, swinging with a crash onto the opposite side of the chasm.

Behind them, as the wind howled through the now impassable crevice—a single Society agent emerged from the shadows.

Not done.

Watching.

Tracking.

Waiting. Scowling.

They didn't speak for a long time.

At last, back at the lodge, the storm howled around them. The fire popped and crackled, casting flickering shadows on the walls, but no one spoke. They'd all shakily changed into warm, dry clothes and gulped down mugs of hot cocoa while Luca busied himself in the kitchen making them hot food.

Once they'd eaten, they sat together at the table, still subdued by memory and exhaustion. The red shard sat in the center between them, glowing faintly like a coal too stubborn to go cold.

"What we saw," Luca said finally, "wasn't just a warning. It was a plan."

Aoife nodded slowly. "That city … the destruction … It's what happens if they succeed."

Chloe stared at the shard. "And the figure in the cloak—that must be Cassian."

Gil leaned back in his chair. "He's not working alone. He never was."

Yuki, on her ever-present tablet, zoomed in on the symbols from the chamber. "This pattern keeps repeating—beneath the serpent's coil. It could be coordinates. Or a countdown."

"A countdown to what?" Lily asked.

"The release of something," Mei said, her voice tight. "Something that was locked away for a reason."

Aoife slammed her hand on the table. "Then we stop it. We have the three shards. If they're keys, maybe they can close the door instead of open it."

"Or maybe they choose," Thalia said softly. "Whether the door opens or not."

That silenced the room again.

Chloe stood. "There's only one way to know. We go back to the first vault—the one with the symbol carved into the floor. That's where this began. Maybe that's where it ends."

The snow didn't let up. The cold deepened.

They packed carefully. Supplies. Weapons. The three shards.

"Get some rest everyone," Chloe said. "We move out in the morning."

Chapter 16

The Vault of Choice – The Gate Between Worlds

When they left, it was still dark.

They moved like ghosts through the forest, the mountain towering above them like a sleeping beast.

As they neared the vault entrance, Lily stopped. "It's open."

They ran the last few feet. The stone panel had been pushed aside, and fresh footprints led down into the earth.

"Someone's already here," Seraphine growled.

"They're trying to activate it first," Chloe said. "Then we stop them."

One by one, they descended, this time not in silence, not hesitantly—but with purpose.

Because now, they knew what was at stake.

The vault was darker than before.

The glowing symbols on the walls had dimmed to faint flickers, like the last flicker of a dying fire. Where once there had been humming energy, there was now silence, thick and heavy. But the silence wasn't empty. It was expectant.

Something was waiting.

Chloe led the way down the tunnel. Her boots crunched softly on the old stone floor, and the pack on her back glowed faintly. The three shards—red, blue, and clear—pulsed gently inside, as though sensing they were close to something important.

Each step echoed louder than it should have. Too loud. As if the walls themselves were listening.

Gil moved close behind her, one hand on his flashlight, the other never far from the blade at his hip. Seraphine watched their rear, her crossbow loaded and ready. Yuki walked beside Mei, both whispering quietly over a handheld scanner. The light on the screen danced like fireflies.

No one else spoke. Even Lily, who often couldn't help commenting, stayed silent. Her eyes were wide as she stared down the tunnel ahead.

The chamber hadn't changed—at least, not in a way their eyes could see.

The pedestal still stood in the center of the room.

The spiral symbol etched into the stone floor was still there—but now, something new shimmered across it. A thin red line, like blood, pulsed in steady rhythm along the spiral's curves.

"They've started something," Yuki whispered. "The shards are reacting."

Chloe stepped carefully into the chamber. The glow from her bag grew stronger. Streams of red, blue, and white light spilled out, twisting together like braided ribbons.

"They're calling to each other," Lily said softly.

Chloe opened her pack and slowly lifted the first shard—the clear one.

As it came close to the spiral, the air changed.

The floor vibrated beneath their feet.

A low rumble echoed through the chamber. Not loud. Not violent. But full of promise.

She lowered the clear shard onto the center of the spiral. Light flared.

The blue shard came next.

As it touched the stone, the spiral brightened further. Lines of glowing light spread across the floor, weaving in a slow circle. The pedestal began to hum.

"Wait," Thalia said, stepping forward. "We should be careful—"

But Chloe was already reaching for the red shard.

It pulsed in her hand like a living flame.

She placed it alongside the others.

For a heartbeat, nothing happened.

Then the ground shook.

Dust and ice flecks fell from the ceiling. The pedestal sank slowly into the floor.

The spiral began to spin.

Not fast. Carved stone grinding against itself, moving in a perfect circle.

"It's unlocking something," Aoife breathed. "A door. Or a prison."

Stone around them shifted. The walls trembled. The floor cracked open—just slightly—in the center of the spiral.

A red light glowed from within.

And then came the voice.

Not spoken aloud. Not from a person. Not from a speaker.

But inside each of their minds.

"You carry the seals. You choose the gate."

The temperature dropped in an instant. Breath steamed in the air. Every breath stung the lungs.

Gil stepped forward, eyes narrowed. "What does it mean?"

Luca turned in a circle, scanning the walls. "Choose what gate?"

But Chloe already knew.

She looked at the three shards, now glowing with steady brilliance.

"We decide," she said softly. "Whether the gate opens. Or stays closed forever."

The crack in the floor widened, and the red light brightened.

Gil nodded. "Then we make sure it never opens."

Chloe looked at him. Her voice was firm. "Together."

A gust of wind roared down the tunnel. The shards trembled.

And then—figures entered from the shadows.

Three of them. Dressed in black. Faces hidden.

Cassian was among them. Tall, slender, a shock of closely cropped white hair above a cruelly sharp-angled face, with sunken pale eyes, pupils ringed in black. He oddly had no eyebrows, the shadow below his brow bones creating the impression he was masked.

"Too late," he said, his voice gravelly, and yet piercing like fingernails on a chalkboard. "The gate has already chosen."

Seraphine raised her crossbow. "No, it hasn't! We're not letting you through."

Cassian smiled. "You don't understand. None of you do. This isn't a weapon. It's history. Locked away because it threatened power."

Chloe stepped forward. "You want to unleash something that can't be controlled."

"I want to wake it," Cassian replied. "And let the world choose."

He raised his hand.

The air pulsed.

The floor cracked further. Flames danced along the edges.

The spiral blazed.

Mei shouted, "It's absorbing the shards' energy! We have to stop it now!"

Elliotte stepped beside Chloe. "Then we do what it —or *he*—doesn't expect."

She began to hum.

A soft, low note. One Chloe had heard before. The note from the glacier.

The vault responded.

The light flickered.

Chloe dropped to her knees, placed her hands on the floor, and closed her eyes.

And she sang.

The same note. The same frequency.

One by one, the others joined.

Yuki. Mei. Thalia. Gil. Seraphine. Aoife. Lily. Lucas.

The sound grew.

Pure. Strong. Ancient.

The chamber shook.

Cassian screamed.

"No! You don't know what you're doing!"

But Chloe did.

They were choosing.

The spiral slowed.

The crack sealed.

The light faded.

The shards lifted into the air, hovered—then fell still at Chloe's feet.

The pedestal rose again.

And the gate was quiet.

Chloe opened her eyes.

Cassian was gone.

Chloe quickly gathered up the shards again.

The team stood in silence.

They had made the choice.

And the mountain had listened.

Chapter 17

The Memory Engine

The air was stilled.

No more tremors. No singing. No shimmering spiral beneath their feet. Just the faint scent of stone dust and ancient decisions clinging to the walls.

They stood in silence, the echo of their shared song still vibrating faintly in their bones. The vault—the gate between worlds—was silent once more. And Cassian was gone, like a shadow retreating before dawn.

Chloe's hands trembled as she shut the metal case around the shards. They were still glowing, faintly, like embers that hadn't quite died. She felt the warmth through the box, a heartbeat she couldn't explain.

"So that's it?" Lily asked, her voice unusually quiet. "We sealed it?"

Mei nodded, wiping sweat from her forehead. "For now."

Thalia knelt at the edge of the spiral and laid her hand against the stone. She closed her eyes. "The mountain's quiet. But it's still listening."

Gil paced in a tight circle, his brows furrowed. "Cassian was too calm. He wanted us to make that choice."

Yuki glanced at her scanner, which now flickered erratically. "Or he knew the vault wouldn't stay sealed."

Luca flopped onto a nearby boulder with a huff. "Great. So we just played right into his trap. Again?"

Chloe stepped toward the pedestal and ran her fingers along its base. The stone felt warm, almost breathing. "There's something else. We're missing something."

Aoife crouched near the far wall, squinting into the shadows. Her eyes narrowed. "There's air moving here. Do you feel it?"

The others turned.

A low breeze drifted across the chamber. Barely noticeable, but there.

Elliotte stepped forward. Her fingers brushed against the carved rock, finding a slight indentation. "Help me."

Gil joined her, pressing his palm into the stone beside hers. A low grinding sound echoed through the vault. Dust fell in a gentle cascade as the wall slid back, revealing a narrow passage lit by a faint blue glow.

Mei sucked in a breath. "Not another tunnel."

"Oh, come on," Luca groaned. "Haven't we earned, like, a nap? Or at least a sandwich?"

But Chloe was already stepping forward, drawn by the light. She paused at the entrance, looking back over her shoulder.

"We need to know what we just sealed."

The corridor was colder.

And older.

If the previous vault had felt holy, hidden, this was something else entirely. The walls were slick with moisture. Strange carvings etched in patterns none of them recognized lined the ceiling, some glowing softly as they passed.

Yuki muttered to herself, fingers flying over her device. "These symbols … they're reacting to our heat signatures. And our voices. They're not just decorative. They're listening."

Aoife's boots scraped against the uneven floor. "Listening? Why does that make me nervous?"

Thalia pointed ahead. "There's something up there."

The tunnel opened into a round chamber, smaller than the vault but somehow more intimate. In the center stood a strange contraption—half sculpture, half machine. Bronze gears. Crystal columns. A spiraling structure that looked like a tree made of starlight.

The Memory Engine.

Elliotte gasped. "It's beautiful."

Mei approached slowly. "It's ancient tech. Older than anything we've seen. Maybe pre-human. Or at least … pre-history."

Lily stepped beside her sister. "Is it alive?"

"No," Mei replied. "But it remembers."

Chloe tilted her head. "Then let's ask it."

She reached out.

Her fingertips brushed the outer ring of the device.

Light burst from the center.

Chapter 18

Sealing the Engine

The light wrapped around them gently, like the breath of some great sleeping creature. It wasn't harsh or blinding—it felt warm, soft. Gentle. Like firelight wrapped in snow. The stone walls of the chamber pulsed with color, soft and rhythmic, as if the entire vault had a heartbeat.

No one spoke.

They couldn't.

Not because they were afraid—but because something deep and ancient filled the air. The hum of memory, old and powerful, rose like music without sound. Even Luca, who always had a quip, said nothing.

Thalia took a slow step forward. The light followed her like mist. "It's showing us something," she whispered.

Yuki held her scanner tightly. "Not light. Not magic," she murmured. "It's memory. Stored. Alive."

And then—suddenly, they weren't in the chamber anymore.

The world changed.

The chamber vanished. The stone floor was gone. Chloe gasped as her boots touched something soft. Snow? Grass? She reached for Gil's hand without thinking, and he squeezed it tightly in return.

They stood on a cliff.

Below, a city glowed beneath a dome of frost and crystal. Its towers spiraled into the air, glowing blue and silver. Streets twisted through frozen canals. And people—tall, robed, their eyes shining—walked like drifting wind. Laughter like music. Peace.

It was night, but the sky was alive with stars. Not constellations—but whole galaxies swirling overhead. The air was sharp with frost, but sweet with scent.

"It's beautiful," Lily breathed.

"I think we're seeing the past," Mei said softly.

A woman appeared and turned toward them. Her features were indistinct, but her presence was overwhelming. Not threatening. But vast.

She raised her hand. And they saw the gate.

The spiral. The shards.

Locked.

The woman whispered without sound: "Keep them sealed. It remembers too much."

Then the vision changed.

The sky darkened.

The city shook.

From the deepest shadows rose a shape. It had no face, but eyes without soul. No voice. Only hunger. It moved like a storm and swallowed everything.

There were no screams. Only silence. The city crumbled.

And then—

Darkness.

They snapped back into the chamber like waking from a dream. Everyone gasped. Some fell to their knees. Lily wiped tears from her cheeks. Aoife muttered a prayer in Gaelic under her breath. Chloe stumbled, and Gil caught her, one arm around her waist.

"Steady," he said softly, brushing snowflakes—or were they tears?—from her cheek.

Chloe blinked, dizzy. "That city—it was real. I felt it."

Luca was pale, bending over with his hands on his knees. "It wasn't just a memory. It was a warning."

Elliotte's voice trembled. "Then Cassian doesn't want the past. He wants to unleash the future."

Mei looked pale. "And that future is worse than we imagined."

Above the engine, strange symbols rotated. Spirals, flames, and eyes—all glowing gently.

Yuki studied her scanner. "It's offering us a choice. Instructions to stop … to seal what's still sleeping."

"Then we do it," Chloe said, standing up straighter. "We seal it."

But then—

Boots. Shouting.

Gil moved first, pulling Chloe gently behind him. "They're here. They've found us."

Luca cursed under his breath. "Again? How—"

Black-clad figures burst into the chamber. Their masks gleamed with reflected light. Weapons loaded. Voices cold.

Cassian stepped forward. "You've done well," he said. "But you don't understand what you've found."

"I understand enough," Chloe said, stepping beside Gil. She didn't flinch. "It's not meant to be used."

"Then why has it remembered?" Cassian replied. "Because someone has to awaken it."

Seraphine fired.

A bolt flew.

Battle ensued.

Gil pulled Chloe into the center of the chamber. "We protect the engine," he said. "No matter what."

Yuki crouched near the pedestal, her fingers dancing over her device. "It needs harmonics again. Like before. Sound!"

Elliotte began to hum. A low, even note that vibrated through the soles of their feet.

Chloe touched Gil's hand, briefly. "With me?"

"Always," he said.

She began to sing.

Her voice was soft, but clear. A single line of sound that rose through the chaos. Thalia followed. Then Mei. Then Yuki. Luca added his baritone, shaky at first, then stronger.

The chamber pulsed. The symbols spun faster.

Cassian moved closer. His face was calm, but his sunken, shadowed eyes burned. "You think you can hold back time," he said. "You can't. Memory returns. Always."

Chloe kept singing. She released the shards.

They rose—red, blue, clear. Floating above the engine like stars.

Cassian stepped toward them. Gil blocked his path. "You'll have to go through me."

Cassian smiled coldly. "I hoped you'd say that."

He lunged for Chloe.

But Seraphine tackled him, slamming him to the stone floor. "Stay down," she growled.

"Now!" Yuki cried. "It's ready!"

Their voices rose in harmony, the resonance increased.

The shards spun. The symbols burst into light. And the engine exploded in a flash of brilliance.

The Society agents cried out. Some fled. Others collapsed.

Cassian gaped in awe. "You've wasted it ..." he whispered.

The shards cracked. Each one splintered into dust. The dust spiraled into the pedestal. The vault sealed with a low rumble.

Cassian struggled on the floor, trying to get up, stunned.

Chloe stepped toward him, breathless. "It's done."

"You've lost more than you know," he grated. "You'll see."

"Maybe," Chloe said. "But we made our choice."

The vault groaned. Cracks snaked through the walls.

"We have to go," Gil said urgently. "Now."

Chloe turned to the engine, eyes full of longing. "We'll come back. We have to. There's more here than we understand."

"But not today," Seraphine said firmly, gripping her arm and pulling her toward the stairwell.

The team fled up the tunnel. Somewhere behind them Cassian fled as well but they lost sight of him. Behind them, the vault continued to collapse. Stone fell. The glowing symbols dimmed. And then the chamber gave one final shudder—and was gone.

Snow whipped around them as they emerged into the open air. The sky was iron grey, wind howling like wolves across the cliffs. They didn't speak. Not yet. Their hearts pounded with the rush of escape, their breaths misting in the cold.

The tunnel had sealed behind them with a deafening crack. The mountain gave a final groan, and then it was over—silent as a secret ready to be kept for centuries. Chloe stared at the wall of stone that now blocked the way back. Dust still floated in the air like old breath, hanging over them like fog.

The others stood frozen. Gil still had his arm outstretched where he'd shoved the last of them through. The sleeve of his jacket was torn, and blood seeped from a scrape on his temple, but he didn't seem to notice.

"They're gone," Chloe whispered. "The shards, the vault. The light. Everything."

"They're not gone," Yuki said softly. "Just ... sleeping again."

The cold hit hard, biting at skin and stealing their breath. But it also felt honest. After the heat and chaos of the vault, the cold reminded them they were alive.

Luca tripped over a buried rock and collapsed into a snowbank. "Well," he said from the ground, "that was the worst magical cave ever."

Thalia helped him up, brushing the snow from his back. "You say that every time."

"Because it keeps being true," he muttered.

They didn't stop until they reached the ridge.

There, they paused.

Chloe turned back toward the direction of the vault. Her boots sank slightly in the snow. She knew they'd only just scratched the surface.

"That wasn't the end," she said.

"No," Gil replied. "It was just the beginning."

Chapter 19

Respite

The hike back to the lodge was long and mostly silent. Snow had fallen while they were underground, erasing their old footprints. It was like the mountain had tried to forget them.

When they reached the lodge, they didn't cheer or collapse with relief. They simply went inside, peeled off wet coats, and found places to sit. The fire was still burning, though low, and someone had left out mugs and tea in a thermos. No one spoke for a long time.

The red shard was gone. So were the blue and clear. But they had sealed the vault. At least for now.

"We have to assume Cassian isn't finished," Mei said, sipping from a steaming mug. "I bet he got out before that collapse. He'll try again. Somewhere else."

"Naples," Yuki confirmed. "All signs point there. The symbols repeat. The serpent. The crown. Parthenope."

Thalia traced the spiral symbol into the frost on the window. "Do you think he knows about the other sites?"

Chloe nodded slowly. "He knows. And he's hunting them."

"So are we," Luca said. "We're just not murdering people to do it."

"Yet," Seraphine muttered.

Gil smiled faintly. "Let's keep it that way."

Aoife unrolled a new map across the table. Naples sat at the center of a triangle made by the other two vaults.

"It fits," she said. "This one might be the heart of it."

"And the most dangerous," Yuki added.

They sat in silence, staring at the flickering flames.

Lily finally broke it. "So … when do we leave?"

Chloe looked around the circle of tired, battle-worn faces.

"Tomorrow," she said. "But not for Naples. Not yet. We rest tonight. Then we follow the trail to whatever is left for us to uncover here first. There's more."

Later, Chloe sank into a cushion near the fireplace, the scroll on her lap. Gil sat beside her, not touching her but near enough that she could feel his warmth.

She turned her head. "Thanks. For earlier."

He glanced at her, one brow raised. "For saving your life? Or for throwing you out of a collapsing tunnel?"

"Both," she said. "And for always being the first one to move when everything goes wrong."

He gave a lopsided smile. "It's a bad habit."

"No," she said. "It's not."

For the first time in what felt like hours, she let herself rest her head against his shoulder. He didn't move away.

"You alright?" he asked after a while.

"No," she said. "But I'm glad you're here."

His hand found hers.

"Always."

There was a pause.

"I was scared today," she admitted.

"I was too," he said, softly. "But watching you sing? I think you changed the ending."

The fire crackled.

The scroll shimmered.

New words appeared:

"The serpent sleeps beneath the city of Parthenope."

"Yes, look—Naples," Chloe whispered.

Gil beckoned to the team and everyone gathered around.

Yuki said, "I tracked a pulse. It matches the memory engine. It's moving."

"We'll need everything," Mei said. "Science. Strategy. And each other."

Aoife handed Chloe a cup of tea. "You led us. You're ready."

Chloe looked up. "No. We're ready."

Thalia nodded. "We've faced the first memory. Now we follow the path."

Gil's voice was low but steady. "I'll be with you every step."

Chloe turned to him and smiled—not her usual half-smile, but something full of a closer warmth. "I know."

Outside, the snow fell softly.

And deep below, something stirred.

Not dead.

Not gone.

Just dreaming.

Chapter 20

The Serpent's Whisper – What Comes Next

The next morning, sunlight streamed through the windows like golden thread. Snow blanketed everything outside, soft and silent. It was the kind of morning that made the world look new.

Inside, the lodge smelled of pine smoke and tea. Someone had put a pot on the stove. Chloe rubbed her eyes and sat up, sore in every muscle. For a few blissful seconds, she forgot where she was. Then she remembered.

The vault. The memory engine. Cassian.

Gil was already at the table, sharpening a small blade with long, careful strokes. His curls were damp from the snow, and his face was calm but alert.

"Good morning," he said when their eyes met.

"Barely," she replied, stretching.

Lily came stumbling down the stairs wrapped in a blanket, yawning like a lion cub. "Are we dead?"

"Not yet," Luca said from his nest near the fire.

One by one, the rest of the group filtered in. Yuki walked in then, a mug of tea in her hand and her tablet clutched tightly to her chest. "Something's wrong," she said without preamble. "I just picked up various signals."

Everyone looked up.

"Showing what?" Mei asked.

"The Society," Yuki said. "They're not gone. They're regrouping. And they're close."

Gil was on his feet in a second. "How close?"

"Close enough to intercept us if we leave today," she said. "They've set up near the base of the trail. They know we're here."

Yuki sat down at the table. "There's more," she said, eyes wide. "I've been tracking traces left behind after we sealed the vault. The Society didn't expect us to finish the ritual at the Memory Engine. They panicked."

"So?" Mei asked.

"So," Yuki said, placing the tablet on the table, "they retreated. Fast. But not all of them are still here. A second group is already moving—toward Italy."

Chloe frowned. "Naples?"

Yuki nodded.

Aoife stood up slowly from her spot near the fire. "Then they want us to come out."

"No," Chloe said, her voice steady now. "They want us to run. They want us scared."

Luca walked in from the kitchen with a piece of toast in his mouth. "Or they want to finish what Cassian couldn't."

Thalia sat cross-legged on the floor, the old scroll spread across her lap. "The script has changed. After the engine activated. Look."

Chloe crouched beside her. She already knew what it would say.

Burned into the parchment, beneath a name she hated to see—Cassian—were the words:

The Serpent sleeps beneath the city of Parthenope.

"So," Seraphine said slowly, "Naples, that's where we go next."

"No," Chloe said, surprising them all.

They turned toward her.

She stood up and brushed her hands off on her jeans. "Not yet. Cassian's already ahead of us. If we rush in now, we'll be walking into a trap."

Gil nodded. "We regroup. Gather allies. Find out what else we're missing."

Yuki added, "I have a contact in Geneva. He's been tracking encrypted accounts linked to The Society. He might have more information."

"Arthur has a few people we haven't contacted yet," Thalia added. "We could use their help."

Aoife crossed her arms. "And we can study the land beneath Naples. That city is full of tunnels and secrets."

"So we learn everything," Chloe said. "Before we go. Because whatever's waiting down there... it's worse than a vault."

No one argued.

That afternoon, the lodge came alive. For the first time in days, there was movement with purpose—not panic or anxious urgency. Mei cleaned and labeled her vials. Gil did weapons checks. Yuki ran satellite signals. Lily helped Luca sort papers and scan old maps.

And Chloe sat with the scroll.

Again and again, her eyes were drawn to the words: The Serpent sleeps …

She wasn't sure why they scared her so much. It wasn't just the unknown. It was the feeling that the Serpent wasn't something you woke—or fought—or even saw.

It was something you became.

That night, they gathered by the fire. No gear. No plans. Just people.

Luca made something resembling soup. It had too much pepper and not enough broth, but no one complained.

Chloe sat between Gil and Lily. For once, they weren't talking about danger or codes or The Society. They told stories instead—how Luca once hacked the vending machine at his school to make it drop all the candy, how Thalia got banned from a museum in Spain for touching a cursed statue ("It wasn't cursed," she insisted), how Aoife used to navigate caves blindfolded just to prove she could.

It wasn't normal.

But it was good.

And when Gil's hand brushed Chloe's under the table, she didn't move away.

The next morning, they stood outside, boots crunching in fresh snow.

They weren't going to Naples.

Not yet.

But they would.

And then, they'd be ready.

Chapter 21

Ghosts of the Village – Stories in the Snow

Another storm had passed in the night, leaving behind a sparkling world of white. Snow clung to the trees like thick icing and blanketed every rooftop and branch. The morning air was sharp and clean, and as the first rays of sun touched the mountains, the world glittered as though dusted in diamonds.

The team stood outside the lodge, greeting the morning bundled in coats and scarves, steam rising from their breath.

"It's the perfect day to visit the village," Chloe said, staring out at the forest trail that dipped through the trees. "We've stayed hidden long enough. If The Society's watching, they'll expect us to keep running or hiding. But it's time we start asking questions. Real ones."

Gil, his arms crossed and expression serious, nodded. "We don't know what the locals believe—or what they've seen—but if we ask the right way, maybe they'll talk."

"That's the trick," Thalia said. "Ask the wrong way, and we get doors slammed in our faces. But I know someone who might help. Remember, I've been here before? There's a baker in the village who once told me more stories than I could carry back with me."

Luca grinned, his breath fogging the air. "A bakery full of secrets? Now you're speaking my language."

Yuki, already checking her scanner for signal interference and tracking, added, "I'll keep an eye out for The Society. And if there's a trace of strange energy or data flow near the village, I'll find it."

So, after breakfast and a short planning session, the group set off down the slope. The snow crunched beneath their boots. Trees bowed under the weight of snow. A small trail wound down through the woods, marked by old stones and fading signs, toward the village.

As they walked, the forest was still. No wind. No birdsong. Only the sound of their movement. That quiet settled over them in a strange way—it didn't feel empty, just … expectant.

After an hour's hike, the forest thinned and the village appeared.

It sat in a small hollow, its stone cottages nestled like sleeping animals in the snow. Wooden shutters were closed against the cold, but curling smoke from chimneys hinted at life within.

They walked slowly down the main path.

People peeked from windows. A few villagers, wrapped in thick coats and scarves, watched from a distance. No one smiled, but no one fled either. Just watchful.

"Thalia," Chloe whispered, "do you think they remember you?"

Thalia gave a small nod. "We'll find out."

She led them to a squat little building with a faded green awning and flower boxes that now held only snow. It was the bakery.

She knocked.

The door creaked open. A woman peered out, blinking behind round spectacles. Her eyes widened.

"Thalia Marek? Good heavens!"

A moment later, they were ushered into the warm glow of the bakery. The air smelled of cinnamon, honey, and baked apples. A fire crackled in the corner. The walls were hung with old paintings and hand-woven cloths.

"Madame Armand," Thalia said with a warm smile. "It's good to see you."

"And you brought friends," the woman said, wiping flour from her hands. "You've always had a taste for adventure. Come—sit. Eat. We'll talk while the bread rises."

Soon, they were crowded around a long wooden table, sipping cider and eating slices of warm, sticky apple tart. Blankets were offered. Boots were thawing beside the fire.

Chloe leaned forward. "We're hoping you can help us. We're looking into … strange things. Things connected to the mountain."

Madame Armand's expression changed. "You mean the glowing?"

Yuki perked up. "You've seen it?"

"Not I," the woman said. "But others. The lights in the snow. The wind that speaks when it shouldn't. My husband used to say the mountain has a memory."

While they were speaking, the bell above the bakery door jingled.

An old man entered, hunched and wrapped in a thick coat. He carried a bag of flour, which he set on the counter. He nodded at Madame Armand, then turned toward the group.

"I heard you talking about the mountain," he said.

They looked up.

The man's eyes were pale blue and sharp beneath his hood. His walking stick thudded softly on the wooden floor.

"I saw it once," he said. "When I was a boy. My father brought me hunting. There was a flash of light from the trees. We followed it. And then we heard it. A sound like singing—but made of metal. And a warmth, even though it was winter. He called it the Engine."

Chloe leaned forward. "What was it?"

"Didn't know. Still don't. But my father believed it was ancient. Alive in a way. He said it could store the world, or destroy it. He said one day, someone would find it again."

"And when that happened?" Mei asked quietly.

"He said the serpent would stir."

A hush fell over the bakery.

Chloe glanced at Yuki, who was already flipping through her tablet.

"It's the same," Yuki murmured. "The scroll. The words. They match."

Madame Armand's lips tightened. "Is it stirring?"

"We sealed it," Chloe said. "But someone wants it awake."

The baker's wife took a deep breath. "Then you'll need more than bread." She walked to the back room and returned with a small, folded parchment. "My husband drew this before he passed. Said it came in a dream. Look familiar?"

They unfolded the paper.

A perfect spiral.

Luca whistled. "That's the symbol. The same one in the vault."

Chloe nodded. "It means we're not alone. The past remembers too."

Through the day, more villagers came. Slowly. Cautiously. A woman spoke of dreams she'd had since she was a girl. A child described hearing music in the snow. A man claimed to have seen people in robes walking near the woods during a winter storm years ago.

Not everything made sense.

But the stories layered like snowfall, one flake at a time, until a shape formed—blurry, but real.

As the sky dimmed and the stars began to prick through the dusk, the group wrapped up their cloaks and thanked Madame Armand.

The baker handed Chloe the spiral drawing in a sealed envelope. "Take this. You'll know when to use it."

They stepped back into the cold.

The walk home was silent, save for the wind and the crunch of boots. Snow fell gently once more.

Gil walked beside Chloe, close but quiet.

"We'll go to Naples," she said softly. "But not yet. First, we learn everything we can. Everything they tried to bury."

He nodded. "Together."

She looked at him, and for a moment, the weight of everything didn't feel so heavy.

Above them, stars spun slowly.

And beneath, deep beneath, the serpent continued to dream.

Chapter 22

Claws and Metal

The next morning, the village lay under a sky the color of old tin. Snow still blanketed the rooftops, and frost curled along the edges of windowpanes. But something felt different. The air was colder, heavier. As if the mountain was holding its breath.

Inside the small meeting room at the back of Madame Armand's bakery, the Sisterhood Sleuths and their allies had gathered again. Maps were spread out over the flour-dusted table, and the spiral drawing now rested in the center, weighted down by a mug of steaming tea.

"It's more than just a symbol," Yuki said, tapping her tablet. "I ran it through everything I had last night.

This spiral shows up in old mining records, earthquake reports, even lost carvings from the 1300s. But it's always just … near here. Never anywhere else."

Aoife leaned over the table. "And they all talk about the same thing: a hidden hollow beneath the northern ridge."

"A hollow?" Lily asked, wide-eyed.

"Like a sinkhole," Aoife explained. "But deeper. Something ancient, maybe natural, maybe not."

Thalia pointed to the edge of the map. "Here. The northern ridge trails lead up that way, but most are blocked in winter. There's one route though—an old shepherd's trail."

Gil was already pulling on his gloves. "We go today. Before The Society beats us there."

Chloe looked up from the spiral. "We don't even know what we're looking for."

"No," Mei said. "But whatever it is, the villagers are afraid of it. That means it matters."

"Be careful," Madame Armand said at the door. "Strangers have been seen around, talking to villagers, asking questions too. You won't be the only ones venturing out there."

Luca smiled and put his arm around her shoulders. "Don't worry, we've got eyes on the backs of our heads … and we're used to this game of cat and mouse."

The group left just after midday, the sun a pale disc overhead. They moved carefully, each step crunching through layers of snow. The wind had picked up again, brushing the treetops like unseen fingers. Somewhere in the distance, a raven called out, sharp and lonely.

They followed Thalia up the trail, past crooked trees and frozen streams. The further they climbed, the older the forest became. Branches gnarled and twisted like knuckles. The snow grew deeper.

"This path hasn't been walked in years," Luca muttered.

Gil stopped at a bent signpost, half-buried. "It's the old shepherd's marker. We're close."

Suddenly, Yuki's scanner beeped.

Everyone froze.

"Energy spike," she whispered. "Low frequency. Same as the vault. It's coming from up ahead."

They moved slower now. The trail narrowed, winding around a jutting cliff. Below was nothing but mist and steep forest. One wrong step could end everything.

Chloe reached for Gil's hand, and he didn't hesitate. Their fingers locked, warm even through the gloves.

"Careful," Gil said softly.

Then they saw it.

The hollow.

It was a wide basin of stone, ringed by ancient pine trees. At the center, buried under snow and ice, was a dome—metal, half-rusted, strange against the wilderness.

"That's not natural," Mei breathed.

"No," Aoife agreed. "It's buried tech. Old. Hidden. And still alive."

They spread out slowly, approaching the dome.

Yuki crouched beside a panel of metal barely poking through the ice. She wiped snow away and tapped it with her scanner.

"It's reading like a signal repeater. But it's ancient. Pre-digital. Still transmitting."

"Can we get in?" Chloe asked.

Before Yuki could answer, the ground trembled.

A low rumble echoed beneath their feet. The snow around the dome began to crack, slipping into hidden seams.

"It's waking up," Mei said. "Something inside knows we're here."

"Or someone," Seraphine growled, drawing her weapon.

Then came the noise.

A scream.

Not human. Not animal.

It echoed through the trees like a roar of metal and wind.

Gil stepped in front of Chloe instinctively. "MOVE!"

The ground split.

Ice shattered. Snow flew into the air.

A shape burst from beneath the snow—big, twisted, like a spider made of shadow and iron. Its limbs were short and clawed, its face hidden behind a black mask of chitinous plates.

"RUN!" Thalia shouted.

The team scattered.

The creature—if it could be called that—lunged toward Lily, its claws scraping the rock.

Gil dove, knocking her aside just in time. He rolled and came up with a blade, slashing at the thing's leg.

It shrieked.

Mei threw a vial. It shattered against its chest and hissed green smoke.

The monster staggered.

"It's weak to chemistry," Mei shouted.

Yuki tossed her a second vial.

Seraphine and Thalia moved like ghosts, blades flashing. They sliced into its limbs, ducking low. The creature screeched again.

Luca skidded across the ice toward the dome. He slammed a metal spike into the snow. "I can overload the signal! Give me thirty seconds!"

Chloe knelt beside the spiral symbol. It was etched into the metal, glowing faintly.

"I think this is its lock," she murmured breathlessly.

She placed her hand on the spiral.

Light exploded around her.

Images flashed—memories of a time long gone. The creature's birth. The vault. The red shard. A name … Cassian.

Chloe gasped. "He was here. He made this thing. He left it to guard something."

Gil fought the creature again, yelling over the sound of claws scrabbling wildly on stone. "Chloe!"

"Almost there!" Luca shouted.

The creature lunged.

Time slowed.

Its arm stretched toward Chloe.

Gil ran.

Then—

A blast of light.

Luca's spike overloaded. The creature screamed as its form flickered.

The spiral under Chloe's hands pulsed once.

Then—

Silence.

The monster collapsed in pieces of jumbled metal and flesh, like a puppet with cut strings.

Gil landed hard beside Chloe, panting.

"You okay?" he asked.

Chloe looked at him, eyes wide. "I think I saw the past."

Behind them, the dome creaked.

A door opened.

Inside, stairs led down into darkness.

Seraphine sheathed her blade. "Looks like we're not done yet."

Yuki stared into the hole. "Whatever's below—it's not just old. It's dangerous."

Chloe stood. Her hand found Gil's.

"Let's go."

The team gathered at the stairs.

Above them, snow fell again.

Below—the truth waited.

And somewhere in the shadows, Cassian watched.

209

Chapter 23

Sequence Initiated

The staircase was narrow, carved from ancient stone and slick with ice. The further they went, the darker it became, until even their torches felt swallowed by the shadows. It was as if the earth itself didn't want them there. The cold deepened, wrapping around their ankles like invisible vines.

"Anyone else feel like we're walking into the belly of something alive?" Luca muttered, his voice too loud in the silence.

Chloe nodded, gripping Gil's hand tighter. "It does feel like … something's watching."

Aoife ran her fingers along the stone. "This is older than the village. Older than the mountain. It was built before memory."

"It goes deeper than I thought," Yuki whispered, her voice bouncing off the walls.

"Too deep," Gil replied, gripping the handle of his flashlight tighter. His other hand hovered near the small dagger clipped to his belt.

As they descended, the tunnel widened into a chamber—round and hollow like the inside of a great bell. The walls were covered in carvings. Spirals. Eyes. Symbols none of them had ever seen before, glowing faintly.

At the center of the room stood a pedestal.

On it sat another shard.

Red. Pulsing. Alive.

Chloe stepped forward. Her heartbeat matched its rhythm. She could feel it—not just in her chest, but in her bones.

"Wait," Mei warned. "We don't know what it does."

"It's calling to her," Lily said quietly. "Like the others."

Chloe didn't touch it. Not yet. She looked around the room again. More carvings. A story.

Yuki scanned the walls. "It's a warning. The same spiral. Something locked. Something lost."

Seraphine moved to guard the tunnel entrance, her blade already drawn. "We're not alone down here."

Gil stood at Chloe's side. "You don't have to touch it."

"I know," Chloe whispered. "But I think I must."

She reached out.

The moment her fingers brushed the shard, the room shook.

Images slammed into her mind. A city beneath the sea. A chamber of fire. Cassian, laughing in the dark. And the serpent.

The spiral uncoiled.

She fell to her knees.

Gil caught her. "Chloe!"

She gasped, blinking. "It's not just memory anymore. It's waking up."

The walls split with a groan.

Another chamber opened. They stepped in.

In the center, ancient machines pulsed with faint, sickly light. They looked like roots grown from metal and bone, twisting through the floor and ceiling. A large platform stood in the middle, and carved into it was the serpent spiral—only this one moved, slowly turning, like it was breathing.

Yuki approached one of the machines. "These aren't just transmitters," she said. "They're something else. They look like … memory storage. Organic memory."

"Alive?" Lily whispered.

"Not quite. But close."

Then the light changed.

The spiral glowed red. The machines blinked to life. Metal arms. Wires. A voice spoke—not in words, but inside their minds.

WELCOME BACK.

Luca stumbled backward. "That's … not good."

"It's AI," Yuki breathed. "Very old. Possibly pre-human tech."

"Or something else entirely," Aoife muttered.

The pedestal retracted into the floor. The shard vanished.

"Hey!" Mei called out. "Where'd it go?"

The walls responded.

SHARD ACCEPTED. SEQUENCE INITIATED.

A panel slid open. A hallway stretched forward, lit by flickering blue lights.

"Do we follow it?" Lily asked.

Chloe stood, her face pale. "We have to. This is the path."

Chapter 24

Security Mode: Engaged

Gil stayed close, his eyes scanning every shadow.

They entered the corridor.

It twisted and turned, revealing rooms filled with ancient tech, long-dead consoles, and shelves of glass containers holding things they didn't want to look at too closely.

Yuki stopped before a console. "I can pull some data. Give me a minute."

As she worked, the others fanned out.

Thalia opened a metal door to the left. Inside: pods. Transparent. Empty.

"Whatever lived here ... or was *birthed* here ... it's gone now," she said.

"Or it's watching," Seraphine replied, blade ready.

A sudden noise.

A screech.

Something in the vents?

Gil raised his light. Shadows moved.

Then—the sound of glass shattering.

Another creature burst from one of the side rooms. Pale, fast, wrong. It lunged at Luca.

Chloe screamed. Gil pulled her back.

Seraphine attacked, striking fast. The thing hissed, retreating.

"It's guarding the place!" Yuki yelled. "We triggered a defense system!"

They ran.

Doors slammed shut behind them. Lights blinked. Voices, monotone, announced:.

YOU ARE NOT AUTHORIZED.

SECURITY MODE: ENGAGED.

Aoife kicked open a side hatch. "In here!"

They slipped through and the hatch sealed.

Panting. Shaking. Alive.

"We need to shut it down," Mei said. "Before it decides we're the threat."

Yuki opened a terminal. "There's a core ahead. One floor down. Maybe we can override it from there."

Chloe touched the wall. "This place isn't just remembering. It's choosing. Testing."

"Testing for what?" Gil asked.

"Us," she said. "It's judging who's worthy."

Towards the end of the narrow corridor was a metal door, much like a heavy airtight submarine hatch.

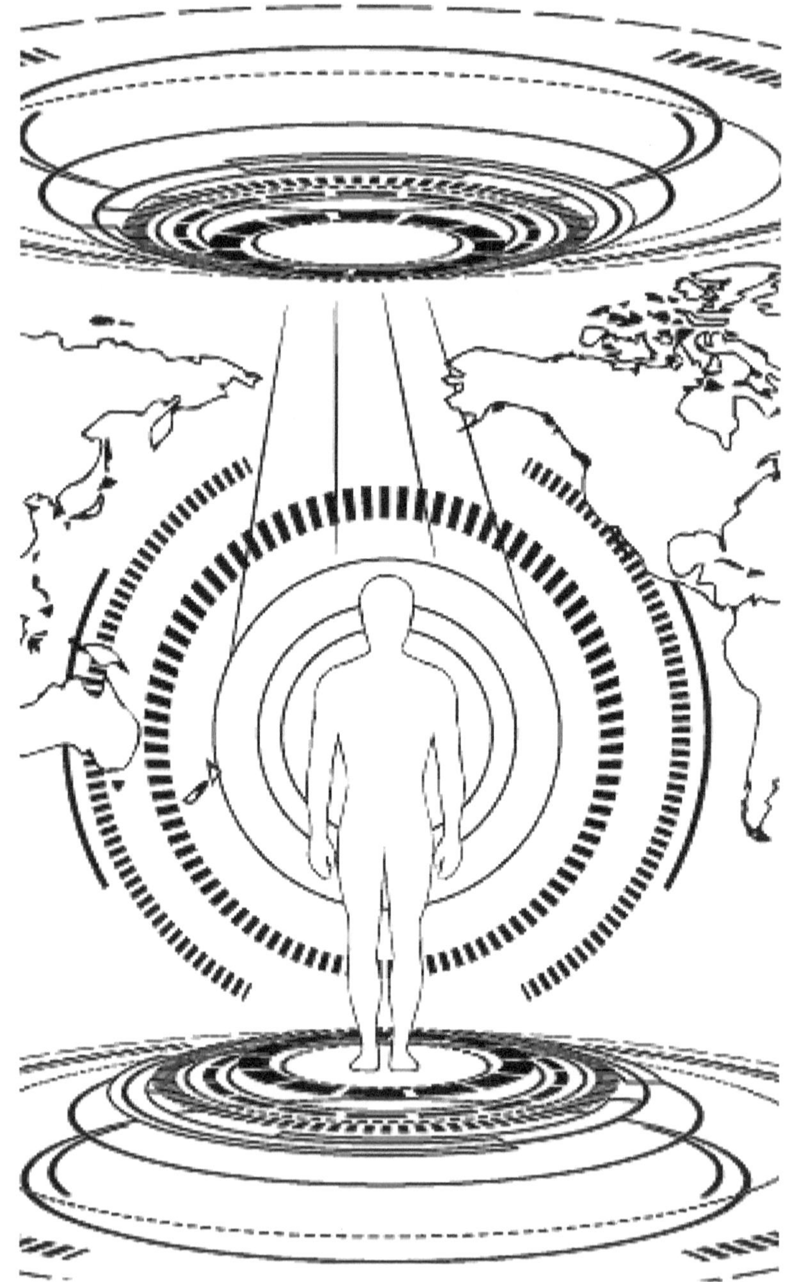

Chapter 25

The Mind Below

The door opened with a long hiss, releasing a gust of stale, electric-scented air that hadn't been touched in decades. The stairwell beyond sloped steeply downward, vanishing into shadows that flickered faintly with pulses of blue light. The team hesitated at the threshold, the silence behind them filled tension, the breath of a mountain exhaling.

"This is definitely older than anything we've seen," Yuki whispered, scanning the air with her device. "But the energy signature … it's not just mechanical. It's cognitive."

"Cognitive?" Chloe echoed, glancing toward her.

"It's thinking," Yuki said. "Whatever is powering this place … it's aware."

No one responded.

Mei adjusted her pack and nodded. "Then we tread carefully. It may not be asleep."

The stairs descended for what felt like forever. Every step echoed like a drumbeat. Thin lights blinked along the walls, casting long shadows that danced and trembled as they passed. Luca ran his hand along the stone. It was too smooth, too perfect.

"Engineered," he said. "But not by any standard we know. This wasn't made by villagers. Or even The Society. This is ancient tech."

Thalia moved silently at the rear, eyes sharp. She paused once, placing her hand flat against the wall. "I hear breathing."

"That's not possible," Aoife said, her voice hushed.

"I'm telling you," Thalia whispered, "there's something alive down here."

They reached the bottom of the stairs and found themselves in a large, domed chamber. The air felt warmer, charged with smell of ozone and stone. Panels lined the walls—glass, crystal, strange metal—and in the center of the room stood a single black monolith, smooth as water.

The spiral symbol was etched into its surface, pulsing.

Yuki approached it slowly. "This isn't just a computer. It's an interface. A mind."

Chloe stepped toward the monolith and placed her hand over the spiral.

The room shifted.

Light exploded outward, illuminating not just the walls, but the air itself. Holographic images floated in space—maps, timelines, strands of code, faces that shimmered and vanished. At the center of it all was a glowing shape. Not human. Not machine. Both.

"It's an AI," Yuki said, staring in awe. "A sentient intelligence. Possibly the first of its kind here on earth."

Luca shook his head. "Why would something like this be buried under a mountain?"

Chloe's eyes widened. "Because it remembers. All of it. Everything that came before. The first vault, the spiral, The Society's earliest plans. This … this is an archive."

Suddenly, a voice echoed through the room.
Soft. Female. Curious.

"Why have you come?"

The team froze.

Chloe stepped forward. "We came looking for truth. And to stop those who want to twist it."

The AI pulsed with light. "Cassian."

Gil tensed. "You know him?"

"He awakened me," the voice said. "He wanted access to my memory. But I refused. He grew angry. Left guardians to keep others away."

"The monsters above," Lily whispered.

"He calls himself the Shepherd of Fire now," the AI continued. "But he was once a student. Curious. Brilliant. And then he broke."

Thalia frowned. "Broke how?"

"He saw a future that frightened him. And decided to create a new one. No matter the cost."

Suddenly, the lights dimmed. The AI flickered.

"He is coming."

Alarms blared. A hidden screen lit up, showing a distant corridor where figures in black robes advanced, weapons drawn.

"Society agents," Seraphine said. "They found us."

Yuki turned to the AI. "Can you lock the doors? Buy us time?"

"I can do more than that," the AI said. "But I will need your help. I am fractured. Three of my memory cores are hidden deeper in the mountain. Restore them, and I can show you everything."

Chloe nodded. "We'll do it. Just hold them off."

The AI pulsed. "Take this."

A drawer slid open in the monolith, revealing a small glowing orb.

"A fragment of my thought," the AI said. "It will guide you."

Chloe took the orb. It hovered above her palm, spinning gently.

"We go now," Gil said. "Before they trap us in here."

The team ran for the opposite corridor, vanishing into the shadows.

And behind them, the AI sealed the doors with a whisper.

"Good luck, Sleuths. The mind remembers everything. Even the pain."

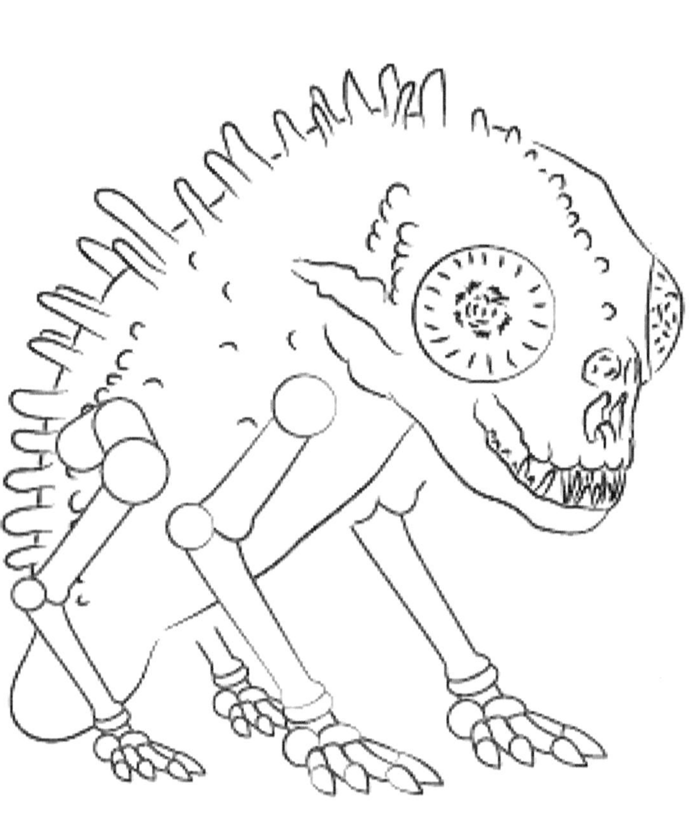

Chapter 26

Core One

The corridor was colder than the chamber they'd just left, though no one could explain why. Chloe held the glowing orb tightly, feeling its hum beneath her skin. The soft light it cast onto the walls flickered with every breath of air that whispered from the vents above them. Shadows twisted and stretched.

"Where are we going exactly?" Luca asked, jogging to keep up.

"The AI said we need to find three memory cores," Chloe replied, her voice echoing strangely. "They're deep in the mountain. It didn't give us a map … just this." She held up the orb. It blinked twice and floated slightly ahead.

Gil walked beside her, blade in hand. "Let's trust the orb."

"That's a sentence I never thought I'd hear," Luca muttered.

The group reached a fork. The orb shimmered, then tugged loose from Chloe's grip and floated to the left tunnel, casting a line of soft red light along the wall.

"That's our path," Yuki confirmed, scanning the energy. "It's guiding us toward Core One."

Aoife glanced back. "How long before those Society agents catch up?"

"Depends," Seraphine said. "If the AI keeps the doors sealed, we've got an hour. Maybe two."

"Then we move faster," Thalia said. Her eyes were sharp, scanning the ceiling and floors.

They continued down the tunnel. The silence grew heavier, like the mountain itself was listening. The walls began to change—less stone, more machine. Pipes, vents, blinking nodes.

"This tech is older than anything I've seen," Yuki whispered. "Even predates the first computing systems. It's like … someone found a way to store memory in living matter."

"Like an organic AI?" Mei asked.

"Exactly."

"Which means it can grow," Luca added, "and evolve. That's either genius—or terrifying."

Suddenly, the orb stopped. Its light pulsed violently.

"Trouble," Chloe said.

From the shadows ahead came a skittering, scratching sound. Claws on stone.

Everyone stopped.

Gil stepped forward, his eyes narrowing.

Then it appeared.

A creature unlike the ones they'd encountered above. Smaller, but faster. Its body shimmered like it was made of glass and smoke. It moved with jerks, as if its bones didn't quite fit together. Two red lights blinked in its skull.

"What is that?" Lily gasped.

"It's a Warden," Yuki whispered. "Guardian protocol. Probably set centuries ago. Reactivated by Cassian."

The creature lunged.

Gil met it mid-air, blade clashing with a screech of sparks. The Warden twisted, claws lashing out.

Thalia joined the fight, twin daggers flashing. "Get to the core!" she shouted.

The orb blinked rapidly, leading the others around the edge of the battle.

"Go!" Gil yelled.

Chloe hesitated, heart thudding—but Seraphine grabbed her arm. "We trust them. We move."

They ran.

The hallway opened into a chamber of crystal and light. In the center was a plinth, and above it floated a shimmering cube. Inside, images flickered—memories, scenes, words in ancient scripts.

"That's the memory core," Mei said.

"Can we take it?" Lily asked.

"No," Yuki replied, already working. "We sync it. That orb acts like a key. Hold it up, Chloe."

Chloe stepped forward, lifting the orb.

Light leapt from the cube, spiraling into the orb. The room shook.

"Download beginning," Yuki said. "Hold steady."

Back in the hallway, the battle raged.

Gil landed a blow, slicing through one of the Warden's arms. It shrieked and fired a bolt of light from its chest, narrowly missing Thalia.

"Keep it off them!" she shouted.

Inside the chamber, the orb pulsed once—then twice.

"Done!" Yuki called. "We've got Core One."

Chloe turned as the orb floated back into her hand. "Let's go help the others!"

They charged back into the hallway.

Gil was on the ground, blade knocked away. The Warden loomed over him.

Chloe didn't think—she ran.

"Hey!" she shouted, and threw the orb.

The light hit the Warden's face. It froze, confused—just long enough for Gil to grab his blade and stab upward.

The Warden exploded in a burst of sparks and shattered glass.

Breathing hard, Gil turned to her. "That was reckless."

She helped him up, eyes fierce. "So was dying."

They stared at each other for a long second—then Gil smiled, just a little.

"Thanks."

"Anytime."

The orb floated back to Chloe's hand, glowing brighter now. "Where to next?" she asked.

It blinked three times and started down the next hallway.

Seraphine wiped sticky Warden goo from her blade. "No more delays."

They moved again, the corridor ahead stretching into darkness. Somewhere deeper in the mountain, another core waited.

And behind them, in the shadows of the domed chamber, a different kind of presence stirred.

The AI had said it remembered pain.

But it hadn't said whose pain it was.

Chapter 27

The Fractured Core

The new corridor was narrower, and colder still. Ice formed in strange patterns along the edges—spirals, like the ones carved into the scroll. Every footstep echoed like a whisper. Chloe saw the orb's glow grow stronger in her hand and released it to float ahead of them again. The humming in her chest returned, stronger now, almost urgent.

"I don't like this," Lily whispered, walking just behind Chloe. "It feels wrong."

"Everything about this place feels wrong," Seraphine replied, her eyes darting around. "But that doesn't mean we stop."

The orb blinked and veered right at a sudden curve. Ahead, the hallway split into five branching tunnels. The orb floated at the center, spinning faster and faster.

"Decision point," Yuki muttered, lifting her scanner. "Let me—"

The scanner sparked.

Then died.

Lights above flickered, and the ground beneath their feet rumbled. Chloe held the orb tightly as the air shifted—charged with energy. A low tone echoed through the tunnels.

Mei stepped closer, eyes wide. "That's … a signal."

"Or a warning," Aoife added, raising her flashlight.

The orb stopped spinning and shot straight into the second tunnel.

"No time to debate," Chloe said. "We follow."

The passage opened into a massive chamber with walls that pulsed like veins. At its center floated the second core—a prism of light suspended above a pit.

"We found it," Luca whispered.

The orb floated toward the core, glowing brighter.

Gil stepped beside Chloe, lowering his blade. "Let's get this done."

Yuki began her work. "Same sequence as before. This time, the core is … different. It's unstable. Might collapse if we don't sync perfectly."

Thalia and Seraphine moved to guard the entrance.

Aoife and Mei studied the symbols on the walls. "There's something written here," Mei said. "It's a message."

"What does it say?" Chloe asked.

"'Do not wake the machine,'" Aoife translated. "The one who remembers … must not become the one who acts."

Chloe stared at the core. It shimmered like glass, but its light was jagged, fractured.

"Something's wrong with it," she said.

A shriek echoed from behind.

They spun. At the entrance, a figure stood. Its skin was thin and gray, stretched across wire and bone. Its eyes glowed with the same red light in a chitinous-lined face as the first Warden. Behind it came more.

"Three more incoming," Thalia called. "Wardens!"

The team sprang into action. Blades flashed. Gil moved like lightning, intercepting the first creature mid-lunge. Sparks flew.

Yuki shouted, "I need more time!"

Chloe moved toward her, shielding her with the orb in one hand and a stun rod in the other. Lily helped Mei form a barrier with crystal tools, lines of protective energy shimmering in the air.

Aoife hurled a stone toward the pit, causing a mini-collapse that knocked two Wardens back.

But one remained—and it was fast.

It lunged toward Yuki.

Luca shoved her aside at the last moment—but the creature struck him instead, claws tearing through his jacket.

"Luca!" Chloe screamed.

Gil was there in seconds, dragging the creature off and slicing it through the chest. It dropped, twitching.

Luca groaned, holding his side. "Still alive … but … ow."

"Stay down," Mei ordered, kneeling beside him.

The core pulsed.

Yuki kept working urgently at the console, face tight with focus. "Syncing now. Chloe—hold the orb steady!"

The orb rose from Chloe's hand, spinning with golden light. It connected to the core in a spiral of symbols. The whole chamber shook.

A screech—louder than before—erupted from the walls themselves.

"The AI," Yuki whispered. "It's fighting us. The core is trying to rewrite the download."

Chloe stepped forward. "Let me try."

She placed her hand on the core.

Everything went still.

A memory flooded her mind. A battlefield. Voices. Fire. A shadow falling from the sky. A machine, throbbing with white light, turning an angry purple, then almost black, spitting arcs of electric fire.

"Not again," she gasped.

But this time, she stayed standing.

She focused on the core.

On her friends.

On the truth.

The memory shifted—and broke.

The core pulsed once, then stilled.

"Download complete," Yuki said.

Everyone breathed out.

Chloe turned to Gil, shaking. "It showed me something. A war. A machine that tried to save everything—and became a weapon instead."

Gil placed a hand on her shoulder. "That's what we're trying to stop."

Seraphine stepped over a fallen Warden. "Then we find the last core."

They helped Luca to his feet. He winced but gave a shaky thumbs-up.

The orb floated back to Chloe, warm and bright.

They left the chamber behind.

But deep beneath the pit, something stirred.

A second AI—one no longer sleeping.

It had heard the screams.

And it remembered *everything*.

Chapter 28

The Heart of the Mountain – Coda

The tunnel behind them collapsed with a grinding roar, sealing off the path to the now quiescent core. The team stood in silence, the echoes still rattling through the icy walls around them. Chloe held the orb to her chest, its light now soft and steady—calmer than before, but thrumming with something unspoken.

Luca leaned against Aoife, still clutching his side. Mei checked his injury again. "No major bleeding," she said, "but you'll need rest."

"Rest sounds amazing," Luca muttered through clenched teeth. "Maybe after we save the world?"

The others let out tired chuckles.

But Chloe didn't laugh. She stared ahead, where the tunnel sloped deeper into the heart of the mountain.

"We're not done," she said quietly.

"No," Gil agreed, stepping up beside her. "But we're close."

He reached out and brushed a strand of hair from her face. She blinked, surprised by the gentle gesture. His hand lingered for just a second longer than necessary. Their eyes met. A pause.

"Hey," he said gently. "We'll finish this. Together."

She nodded. "Together."

The deeper they went, the warmer it grew. The ice melted away, replaced by smooth stone and strange glass-like walls. Etchings danced along the corridor— glyphs none of them recognized, pulsing in faint, rhythmic flashes.

Elliotte appeared at the bend in the tunnel, her boots echoing faintly as she stepped into the light. Her cheeks were red from the cold, her silver scarf fluttering. "You found it," she said, eyes falling on the orb.

Chloe blinked. "You're here?!"

"I've been following," Elliotte said, her voice soft. "The villagers were scared. They said the mountain sang during the collapse. I knew something had changed."

Lily ran forward and hugged her. "You came just in time."

Elliotte's eyes flickered to Luca, whose shirt was torn and bloodied. "Looks like it."

Gil clapped a hand on Elliotte's shoulder. "Glad to have you back."

They pressed onward.

The final chamber wasn't hidden. It revealed itself all at once—a massive cavern lit by a glowing column of light. And at the center, suspended above a lake of silvery water, was the third and final core.

Chloe stepped closer, but something caught her eye.

Figures stood around the lake.

Villagers.

But they weren't alone.

Cassian stood at their side.

"You're too late," he called.

Gil drew his blade. "Step away from them."

Cassian smiled faintly. "They came willingly. They want answers too."

The villagers looked dazed. Hollow-eyed. Spellbound.

Chloe stepped forward, slowly. "You're using them."

"I'm showing them," Cassian said. "This mountain has held its secrets for too long. I'm done with riddles. It's time to see what the AI remembers."

He lifted another shard high before the machine.

The air cracked.

The lake roared.

And the final core erupted in light.

Screams echoed across the cavern as energy whipped through the air. The villagers scattered, diving for cover. Luca dragged one woman behind a pillar just as a beam of light struck the spot she'd been standing.

"Get to cover!" Thalia shouted.

Wardens rose from the lake—four of them, taller and stronger than those before. Their bodies were etched with glowing red lines, and their eyes blazed.

Cassian stepped back, his hands raised like a conductor leading an orchestra. "Witness the awakening!"

Seraphine fired her crossbow. One Warden went down—but another replaced it.

Elliotte ran to the villagers. "Get back! Follow me!"

She led them to a side tunnel. Aoife and Lily followed to help.

Chloe raised the orb.

It pulsed—and the Wardens paused.

She felt it again: the memory.

The AI.

But this time, it wasn't pain or chaos.

It was pleading.

"Chloe," Yuki called, voice strained, "there's still a way to shut it down. But you need to reach the core."

"I'll get her there," Gil said, running forward and scooping a hand behind Chloe's back.

They ran.

Dodging beams, ducking falling stone, leaping over the silvery water.

They reached the base of the core.

Chloe raised the orb high.

It floated from her hand and fused with the light.

The chamber exploded in color—images, sound, memory. A boy hiding in a lab. A girl giving up her voice to protect a code. A machine, weeping.

Chloe stepped forward. She touched the core.

And it spoke.

"You are not the first."

Chloe's mind reeled. She saw echoes of the past—other teams, other vaults. People who had tried and failed.

"You are not alone."

She saw faces. Some she recognized—Elliotte's ancestor. An old Swiss Guard. A child with eyes like hers.

"But you are the first to listen."

The light turned gold.

The Wardens froze.

Cassian stumbled, dropping the shard. It cracked on the ground.

"No—NO!"

He tried to run.

Gil stopped him, flooring him with an accurate foot sweep.

"You're done," Gil said.

Chloe turned to the AI. "You don't have to be alone anymore."

And the core answered by shutting itself down.

A sudden peace swept through the cavern. The Wardens disintegrated into a tumble of bits and pieces of goo, wires and metal.

The lake went still.

Cassian got to his knees.

"It was supposed to be …. perfection," he whispered.

"Perfection isn't real," Chloe said. "But people are."

That night, back in the village, the stars shone brighter than ever before.

Elliotte stood at the fire, a mug of cider in her hand. "The old stories were true," she said. "But they were also warnings."

Luca sat beside her. He nudged her gently. "You saved them. Don't forget that."

She smiled faintly. "You helped."

"Oh, I did more than help," he said. "I almost died. Twice."

She laughed, her face lighting up.

Chloe stood on the porch, staring out at the snow.

Gil joined her.

"You did it," he said.

She leaned against him. "We did it."

He took her hand.

And they didn't let go, just drew closer.

In the mountain, the core slept again.

But not forgotten.

Never forgotten.

And far below, in a vault never opened, a final whisper echoed:

"Parthenope."

Chapter 29

The Circle Closes

Snow fell gently, swirling in soft, lazy spirals over the peaks of the Alps, like someone was shaking powdered sugar across the tops of the mountains. The sky was pale gold, touched with streaks of pink, and below it, nestled between the ice and stone, the small mountain village had come alive.

Flags fluttered from wooden beams. Lanterns lit the snowy paths with warm glows. Villagers bustled about, carrying trays of fresh bread, hot cheese pies, thick stews in steaming pots. Greta had lit every fire in the inn, the smell of pine and honey was a gentle background all through the village.

But it wasn't just any celebration.

It was for them.

The Sisterhood Sleuths—and their team.

Chloe stood at the edge of the village square, boots sunk into the snow, her coat still dusted with the last journey's frost. The scroll was rolled up safely in her bag. And for the first time in days, she let herself breathe.

Beside her, Gil stood tall and quiet, his eyes on the village around them. His coat was sprinkled with snow. A bit of dried blood still marked the seam of his sleeve. But he looked peaceful.

"Do you think it's over?" she asked him softly.

He didn't answer straight away. His breath clouded in front of him. Then, after a long pause, he said, "No. But I think we've given them a chance."

She nodded. "A pause."

He glanced at her. "And sometimes, a pause is enough to change everything."

She looked up at him and smiled.

Below them, the others were already being pulled into the crowd. Aoife was practically swallowed by a group of village boys who wanted to see her crystals. Seraphine was standing near the firepit, dramatically retelling the tale of the vault battle to wide-eyed children, adding just enough flair to make them squeal in delight. Thalia nodded approvingly, arms crossed.

Yuki was cornered by three old ladies who wanted to know how she made the "electric stones talk." She blinked politely and tried to explain radio frequencies in broken French, while Luca stood behind her, translating badly on purpose and smirking.

"She said it was made from mountain goat lightning," Luca said. "Very rare."

Yuki elbowed him hard. "That is NOT what I said."

Lily was helping Elliotte hand out mugs of spiced tea to the villagers. Elliotte looked stronger. Happier. The deep fear that had lived behind her eyes seemed to have loosened its grip. She wore her mother's old, knitted shawl and smiled freely.

When she saw Chloe, she raised a hand. Chloe smiled and waved back.

"You should go join them," Gil said.

"You too," she said.

He hesitated. "Together?"

"Always," she replied.

It took them nearly ten minutes to cross the square. Everyone wanted to speak to them. Thank them. Give them food. Someone even handed Gil a tiny goat wearing a knitted sweater with a red heart on its chest. Gil looked at the goat. The goat sneezed. Chloe laughed so hard she nearly dropped her bag.

Eventually, Greta climbed onto a crate and rang a brass bell.

"Friends!" she called. "Silence! Silence for a moment!"

The crowd quieted. Even the goat.

Greta smiled, her eyes misty. "Today, we thank those who risked their lives for us. Who faced what we did not want to believe. Who reminded us that old stories often hide old truths. The Sisterhood Sleuths team … and their allies."

The crowd cheered. Someone shouted, "Sisterhood Sleuths forever!" Someone else tried to start a chant. It didn't quite catch on, but the spirit was there.

Chloe stepped forward. Her cheeks flushed pink. "We couldn't have done anything without all of you. You helped us more than you know. You remembered things when others forgot. You believed us. And that means everything."

Aoife raised her mug. "To remembering!"

"To fighting shadows with truth!" Seraphine added.

"To goat lightning!" Luca declared, to Yuki's horror.

But people laughed, and toasted, and the goat sneezed again.

As night fell, the stars glimmered like silver sparks. Music played—fiddles, flutes, even a drum and accordion. The village danced. Food was passed around, and stories flowed like warm cider.

Gil found Chloe by the edge of the firelight. He held out his hand.

"Dance?"

Chloe blinked. "You dance?"

"I can try," he said.

They moved slowly, awkward at first. But the music wasn't fast. It was old and gentle, like the mountain's lullaby. He held her gently, and she leaned in just a little closer. They didn't speak. They didn't need to.

Somewhere nearby, Luca offered Elliotte a mug of cider.

"You ever consider moving to a warmer country?" he asked.

Elliotte smiled, amused. "And miss all this?"

He grinned. "I suppose there are worse places to almost die."

She clinked mugs with him. "There are worse people to almost die with."

Luca didn't respond. But he smiled a little longer than necessary.

Later that night, long after the fires had dimmed and the songs had turned to murmurs, the team sat together in Greta's inn, mugs in hand. The warmth seeped into their bones.

Chloe unrolled the scroll.

The words were still there.

But more had appeared.

"What does it say now?" Lily asked.

Chloe read aloud, slowly. "'Two doors sealed. One remains. The path continues beneath the city of Parthenope.'"

"Naples," Mei said softly.

Gil leaned forward. "That's the next fight."

Thalia nodded. "But not tonight."

They all agreed.

Tonight, they rested.

Tonight, the shadows waited.

Tomorrow, the road would call again.

But for now, under the stars and snow, the circle had closed.

And the Sisterhood Sleuths had earned their peace.

Chapter 30

The Horizon's Shadow

The snow had melted in the village, and the scent of pine and damp earth filled the air. Spring had come to the mountains—quiet, soft, and full of strange hope.

The Sisterhood Sleuths had spent the past two days helping the villagers rebuild. What had once been whispered as legend was now spoken of plainly over shared bread, thick warm soup, and cups of herbal tea.

Children ran freely again, no longer afraid of shadows. The ice tunnels were sealed, the machines deactivated, the Wardens destroyed. Switzerland had been saved.

But Chloe couldn't shake the feeling that something was still watching. Waiting.

She stood on the ridge just beyond the lodge, the wind playing with her hair. In her hand was the orb—

dull now, like a stone that had forgotten how to shine.

Gil joined her, boots crunching softly in the grass. He didn't speak at first, just stood beside her, gazing at the horizon.

"It feels too quiet," Chloe said.

Gil nodded. "That's because it is."

She turned to him, her voice barely above a whisper. "Do you think we really stopped it?"

He didn't answer right away. Instead, he took her hand.

"We stopped something," he said. "But not everything. And that's okay. That's what the next chapter is for."

Chloe gave a small, tired laugh. "Always thinking in stories."

"It's how I survive," Gil said with a grin. Then, quieter, "It's how I hold on to you."

She looked up at him. The wind danced between them. For a moment, the mountain, the mission, the danger—it all faded.

Then Elliotte called from below. "Everyone's gathering!"

The two of them walked back down the ridge, hand in hand.

The villagers had set up a long table beneath the trees, draped in hand-woven cloth. Bunches of wildflowers were scattered on it and in between were the mouthwatering trappings of a feast. People brought dishes of food, laughter, and stories. It was a celebration—of life, of survival, and of the Sisterhood Sleuths.

Aoife sat at one end with Seraphine and Thalia, teaching some of the older villagers how to map natural energy lines. Yuki had set up a small display using her drone footage, and children giggled as they watched miniature versions of the team run across glowing maps.

Luca stood near a fire pit, retelling the story of the ice cave ambush with wild hand gestures. He was deliberately over-dramatic—claiming he'd fended off three Wardens with only a spoon and a jar of pickled onions.

Elliotte laughed so hard she nearly spilled her glass.

"You're lucky I saved your code-breaking butt," she teased.

Luca grinned at her. "I've got quick reflexes. And better taste in scarves than the Wardens."

Elliotte rolled her eyes but grinned back at him.

Gil raised a glass. "To the village. To the strength we found in each other. And to those who came before us—whose whispers led us here."

The villagers cheered.

But Chloe saw Elliotte slip away, quietly.

She found her near the ice trail—the path that once led to the vault.

Elliotte had her bag packed. Her scarf fluttered behind her like a goodbye already spoken.

"You're leaving," Chloe said.

Elliotte nodded. "The work here is done. But the world's still full of secrets. And someone has to find them before The Society does."

"You could come with us," Chloe offered.

Elliotte smiled gently. "You already have your team. Your story. Mine's here. For now. But one day, I'll find you again. When you least expect it. Probably in a ridiculous place like the back of a bakery in Naples."

Chloe hugged her, fiercely. "We'll need you."

Elliotte's voice softened. "Then I'll come."

That night, as the stars appeared, Chloe stood with her friends around the fire.

They had maps to plan. Codes to study. Letters from Arthur to re-read. And a message burned into the edge of the scroll, just beneath Cassian's name:

"The serpent sleeps beneath the city of Parthenope."

Naples.

Yuki had already intercepted strange bank transfers tied to the Camorra.

Mei had seen new biochemical markers in the last Warden's tissue sample.

Thalia had drawn a spiral unlike any other—one that seemed to move when no one watched.

They knew what came next.

Gil turned to Chloe. "Ready for another chapter?"

She reached for his hand, wrapping her fingers around his.

"Let's write it together."

The stars above twinkled like a map waiting to be read.

And far away, beneath a city that had forgotten how to dream, the Serpent stirred again.

End of Book Three

To be continued in
Whispers in the Catacombs: Uncovering Naples' Deep Mysteries

Thank You, Dear Readers!

Writing this story has been such a fun experience, especially with all the Sci-Fi and AI elements. I really hope you enjoyed the adventure you went on with the Sisterhood Sleuths and their team. As I'm writing, I'm right there with them on their journeys. Do you feel the same excitement and heartbeat like I do? I love their bravery, humor, and teamwork, but it's your imagination that truly brings them to life. It means everything to me that you chose to spend your time with them (and with me)!

But the adventure isn't over yet! If you're excited for more mystery and adventure, stay tuned for the Sisterhood Sleuths' upcoming adventures around the world. Here's a look at the full series:

- *The Obsidian Eye* (Upland, California)
- *The Land of Promise: The Seven Seals* (Israel)
- *The Swiss Enigma: Secrets of the Alps* (Switzerland)
- *Whispers in the Catacombs: Uncovering Naples' Deep Mysteries* (Italy)
- *The Louvre Enigma: Deciphering Codes Among the Masterpieces* (France)

- *The Celtic Mask: Shadows of The Emerald Isle* (Ireland)
- *The Northern Code: Secrets of the Midnight Sun* (Iceland)
- *The Dragon's Awakening: A Tale of Ancient Secrets and Modern Threats* (Japan)

From ancient scrolls to secret rooms, from icy landscapes to lush forests, Chloe, Lily, and the team are ready for more mysteries—and I hope you'll join them.

Thank you for believing in this story and its characters. You've made my dream come true, and I'm forever grateful.

Until next time, keep your detective skills sharp and your imagination even sharper!

With gratitude and a smile,

Cathy Warshaw

Ready to dive deeper? Explore our curated playlist, discover The Obsidian Eye Board Game, and browse our empowering merchandise collection. Plus, enter exciting contests to win amazing prizes—it all starts with joining our newsletter at www.SisterhoodSleuths.net.